Slippery Saturday

A Tabitha Chase Days of the Week Mystery
(Book 4)

Denise Jaden

Slippery Saturday

A Tabitha Chase Days of the Week Mystery (Book 4) By Denise Jaden

A WINTER SOLSTICE FESTIVAL, a dangerous high-wire act, and a premeditated murder.

Tabby is excited for the Winter Solstice Festival, where she plans to gently introduce her younger sister to the magic of Crystal Cove. But when the local witches act evasive rather than friendly, and when one of them falls to her death from a high-wire act that appears to have been rigged, Tabby has no choice but to give her sister a crash course in magic-led sleuthing.

All clues lead to a surprising suspect, but when it appears this death could be connected to a long-ago tragedy, Tabby may be too emotionally involved to see the truth.

Will she be able to harness her gifting and catch the killer?

Chapter One

The Heirloom Café was abuzz on Saturday afternoon for the upcoming solstice festival. I was at least as excited as the group of witches lined up for their caffeine-to-go, but my anticipation had nothing to do with their latest festival.

My sister Pepper was coming for a visit, and should be here any moment.

I did my best to quell my perma-grin and took the order of the next witch in line. When I rang in Ruth's Mocha Cookie Crumble, Katie, the barista who had just come on shift, slid two paper cups in front of me.

Katie had ultra-neat handwriting, and I attributed it to her still being in eleventh grade. I read the notes from the cups and called them out.

"Sheena? Here's your Beet Latte." I was particularly proud of this coffee creation. While it didn't taste as unique as it sounded, it was delicious. As Sheena moved up through the line to get her drink, I read the other name. "Juliana?" This was one of the witches I didn't yet know by name, so I tried to commit her blonde hair and blue eyes to memory as she retrieved her drink.

"I'm sorry I'm late, ladies!" Marigold Weathers swept into the café and the vibe immediately took on a frantic nature. The line cleared and she made her way toward the counter. She was known as the Queen Witch of Crystal Cove, and while she had made some poor decisions in recent months that had most of the town unsure of how they felt about her, the witch crowd still quickly fell in to her authority without a second thought.

"Americano with cream?" I asked, as she approached me. She usually only purchased the cheapest coffee on the menu, but on special occasions, I knew her to splurge for an Americano.

She brightened at my quick knowledge of her, but as I passed her order along to Katie, I couldn't see anyone else but the girl in the doorway.

"Pepper!" I practically squealed.

I raced around the counter, leaving Katie to take over. In truth, my shift was already finished. I had been helping her get through the rush while I waited for Pepper, who now pulled me into a hard hug. "Tabby Chase! It's been way too long!"

Pepper had called me by my full name since we were kids. I think it started when our dad had yelled at me, calling me by my full name in admonishment, and Pepper had been too young to realize she probably shouldn't have mimicked his words. Except when Pepper said it, even to this day, it came out as one word. *Tabbichase!*

When I'd first arrived in Crystal Cove, I'd gone to great effort to hide my last name and my relation to the state senator from the locals, but I soon learned that no one here cared. The Crystal Cove locals cared a lot more about the type of person you were than what family you'd come from. However, feeling Pepper's infectious energy, I couldn't wait to introduce her around and claim her as part of me.

Over her shoulder, I could see that things had gone tense among the witches since Marigold's arrival. "...another death threat on my car," I heard her tell the others with a serious gleam in her eyes. "I really need all of you to keep an eye out tonight," she added.

Did she say death threat? I could barely pay attention to what Pepper was saying.

"Even the drive here was freeing," she told me with her arms wide. Under her wool coat, she wore a blouse and slacks and I wondered if she'd come straight from campus, without even stopping at our parent's house. She was in medical school, which had been her dream, but her schooling had been a struggle the last several months. "I can't tell you how happy I am to be out of school and away from Dad's questions." She looked around the café. "You may have trouble getting rid of me, Sis."

While a big part of me wouldn't mind my sister staying indefinitely, I knew this wasn't what would ultimately make her happy. She and my older brother Zach had been born with the driven gene. Neither of them would survive living in slow-paced Crystal Cove for more than a few days.

"I'd be happy to have you," I told her, regardless.

Before I could move us closer to the witches, introduce Pepper around, and ask Marigold what she was talking about with a death threat, the whole group of them moved toward the door.

Only about half of them had coffees in their hands, but Marigold was saying, "We really need to get busy if we're going to have everything ready for seven o'clock."

I watched them go, wondering if Marigold had been serious about receiving death threats. Had she told the police about them? I could always ask my detective-friend, Jay. Or at the very least, I could mention to him what I'd overheard, just so he could keep his ears open as well.

Then again, part of me wondered if this was just another stunt of Marigold's—something to bring on some extra drama to keep the witches focused on her agenda for the upcoming festival.

There were still a couple of people left in line at the counter, so I told Pepper, "Just give me a second. I'll help Katie finish up and I'll make you a hot drink to go. You still like gingerbread lattes?"

She grinned. "My favorite!"

I directed her to a chair and raced behind the counter.

"That's your sister?" Katie asked, in between taking orders.

Out of convenience, we had switched places. Katie was now ringing in orders, and I quickly looked over her notes to get busy on the Espresso machine. This was better, anyway. Katie wasn't a huge fan of the witches, but now that they had cleared out, she was more comfortable with the customers remaining. She had been finding her footing with many of the other locals and knew more of them by name than I did, even though she'd only lived in Crystal Cove for three months.

"Yes, that's Pepper. I'll introduce you when we're through this rush."

It only took another three orders, and we were on top of it. People were eager to get home for dinner before the festival tonight.

I beckoned Pepper over. "Katie, this is my sister Pepper. Pepper, this is my favorite barista, Katie."

"How many baristas are there in this town?" Pepper asked, jokingly, and then added, "Nice to meet you, Katie."

Katie asked Pepper about medical school, the awe evident in her voice as I headed to the back room to retrieve my purse. When I returned, they were on the subject of the witches.

"I mean, I guess they're real witches, but it's not like I've ever seen them perform any magic," Katie was saying.

"So strange. I've had a hard time believing the stories Tabby's been telling me about witches here until I saw them." The interest in my sister's voice was surprising. I hadn't told Pepper much regarding the local witches. I'd always thought of the rest of my family to be too rooted in realism to have any interest in the underlying magic of Crystal Cove, but now both my mother and my sister had surprised me.

"If you stay for any amount of time, you'll definitely get to meet them," Katie went on. "If you want to, that is. They're pretty cliquey, if you ask me."

I didn't know why, but Katie warning Pepper away from the witches bothered me. Maybe because some of them had become my friends. Rachael Adams, while she wasn't terribly skilled with magic, had become a good friend. But Katie wasn't completely off base, either. Many in the local witch population acted standoffish to those who weren't firmly in their coven.

Whatever the reason, I spoke up. "Ready to go? Let's go get you settled on the *Lady of Fortune* for your stay."

Before I rounded the counter, Katie switched subjects, and asked, "Hey, do you know about a surveyor that was supposed to be here at the café today?"

"Surveyor? No, why?" I grabbed my latte and took a sip.

Katie shrugged. "There was some guy outside taking measurements a couple of hours ago. He didn't come inside, and I didn't get a chance to go out and ask him why he was here."

"What did he look like?" This definitely seemed odd, especially if he hadn't come inside. Then again, it could be he was hired by Olivia for something and when he didn't see her behind the counter, he didn't bother to stop in.

Katie shrugged again. "He was wearing a baseball cap, so I couldn't see his face. He was in a navy suit."

A suit with a baseball cap? Then again, I barely had a better grip on the Crystal Cove locals than Katie.

"I'm sure Olivia knows about it, but you can mention it when she comes in to lock up, to be sure." I waved to her. "Have a good night."

She said the same thing back to us and we headed out the door.

It was only a short drive to the marina, but Pepper spent the three blocks gazing out the windows in awe. "I can't believe this is your home now."

It was definitely a far stretch from Portland. As she followed me down the wharf, Frank, the marina owner, and another man were chatting near the office. Or, as I moved closer, I wondered if they were arguing.

"I swear, I'll pay the rest off by the end of the year," the man I didn't know said. His jeans were worn and he wore a thick red and black plaid jacket. He looked like a fisherman.

"That's only a little more than a week, Henry," Frank told him. "After January first, I can't keep it for free."

I slowed up, not wanting to eavesdrop, but also wanting to introduce Frank to Pepper, since she would be staying on my houseboat for a few days.

"I said I'd have it!" The gruff man spun on his heel and almost knocked into me and Pepper as he marched for the marina's parking lot. I grabbed Pepper's arm, as she wasn't as used to the instability of the wharf.

Once I had us both righted, I said, "Frank?" before he disappeared into the marina's office. He was usually more outgoing when new people visited the marina, but I guessed he was distracted. "Everything okay?" I asked, before introducing my sister.

He turned back with his brow furrowed, but just now seemed to see that I had company and pasted on a smile. "Oh, yeah, yeah. Just another guy struggling to pay for his slip. I'm pretty sure the guy has a gambling problem." He sighed. I'd seen him have to evict a boat owner who hadn't paid a couple of months ago, and I could tell it was the one part of the job Frank hated.

But then he seemed to shake off the stress of it and extended a hand. "Is this the sister I've been hearing so much about?"

"Yes, this is Pepper. She'll be staying..." I trailed off, as Pepper still hadn't given me a clear answer on how long she planned to stay.

"...On our aunt's boat," Pepper finished for me. "*The Lady of Fortune*, right?" She looked between us.

Frank smiled. "Any family of Lizzie's—" he glanced at me "—and Tabby's, is welcome here."

As Pepper followed me across the gangplank onto the *Lady of Fortune*, Sherlock, my late aunt's cat, watched us through his spectacles from the front deck with interest. Pepper didn't seem to notice him, and while Sherlock could communicate with me with mind-speak, that particular talent didn't go both ways, so I tried to indicate with my eyebrows and smile that Pepper was family and he could trust her.

However, he stayed out on the cold deck while we went inside.

But then I let out a huff of a laugh under my breath when I saw that during my shift at the café, Sherlock had pulled a dozen detective novels out of their piles and onto the floor of the houseboat.

"Sorry about the mess!" I rushed ahead to sweep them back into piles. While Sherlock could be helpful in solving investigations using these books, I often thought he just made a mess of them as a means of getting attention, like a toddler acting out. I couldn't very well explain that to my sister, at least not yet, so instead I made up a vague excuse. "I was just reorganizing a little before you got here."

She didn't seem to notice the mess and instead went straight for the galley, where she helped herself to a glass from the cupboard, as though she'd been in the boat's small kitchen a hundred times, and opened my small fridge to pour herself some juice.

"You can stay in Aunt Lizzie's room." I motioned toward the door that led to the upper deck of the houseboat. I had hoped one of the neighboring houseboats may have been free when Pepper came for a visit, but I hadn't known how popular the winter solstice festival would be. Every houseboat and bed and breakfast in the area had been reserved months ago.

"Where will you sleep?" Pepper looked around and I motioned to the camping mat I kept folded in the corner. After Mom's visit and trying to make the couch cushions work on the floor, I'd decided to stop by Happy Hardware to find a more comfortable solution.

As kids, whenever we went away as a family, Pepper and I usually slept in a hotel bed together, while our brother took the floor. It felt a little strange, offering Pepper the bed on her own, but we were both adults now, and the upper cabin would be pretty cramped for two people.

She stared at me for a long second, then placed her empty juice glass on the counter grabbed for her suitcase and headed up the stairs.

"I wanted to take you to a festival tonight, so put on something warm and comfortable," I called.

While she was gone, I washed her glass and filled Sherlock's food dish. Out of the corner of my eye, I caught movement as my cat crept toward the stairs.

"No, Sherlock," I told him. "My sister's up there for the weekend. Remember?" I had told Sherlock this several times in the last week, plus he'd seen me cleaning up the room and moving some of my clothes to a downstairs closet to make room for her. Then again, my cat tended to have a selective memory.

Either that or his kitty rebelliousness made him automatically want to do whatever I'd told him not to.

"We're leaving the upstairs for Pepper." I added again.

I didn't think Pepper was allergic to animals, but we'd never had any pets, and I honestly didn't know how she'd react to having a cat aboard the boat with us. Sherlock headed for his kibble, and that was when I noticed he'd knocked over another pile of detective novels.

I rolled my eyes and went to restack them, wondering what Pepper would think if she saw my cat in the act of tossing books around the living space. Then again, I'd never actually *seen* Sherlock actually move the books from their stacks. It always happened when I wasn't watching, and part of me still wondered if it was the cat, or if it was the magic-infused houseboat I lived on.

When I turned back around, Sherlock was gone. I sighed and rolled my eyes, about to go up the stairs after him, but before I could, Pepper appeared in the doorway.

"This is so cute!" She held up a navy dress with tiny white polka dots that I'd never seen before. "Can I borrow it for tonight? I'll wear it with some leggings underneath for warmth."

I forced a smile and a nod. It wasn't the first time my late aunt's houseboat had delivered new clothes to my closet, but how was I going to explain these magical *happenings* to my very reality-brained sister if they kept happening?

She disappeared back up the stairs, calling, "And your cat is so sweet!" as she went.

Sweet? Sherlock? He was clearly up to something.

I sighed to myself, hoping I could break the idea of magic to my sister gently, before he started mind-speaking to her, too.

Half an hour later, I had put on a dress with leggings to complement my sister's and we were headed out the door.

If anything would introduce my sister to the magic of Crystal Cove, it would be the witches' winter solstice festival.

Chapter Two

SHERLOCK DIDN'T ASK FOR permission before trailing us up to the main road. The bulk of the festivities were along the water, well within walking distance.

"You're letting the cat come along?" Pepper's interested gaze landed on Sherlock, who was scampering along behind us. "He's allowed out?"

I held back a balk at her question. Ever since I'd known Sherlock, he'd pretty much made his own rules. There was really no explaining that the word "let" wasn't within Sherlock's quite extensive English vocabulary, so I told her, "We won't be going far. He can find his way back."

This seemed to satisfy her. As we moved along Shoreline Drive, which actually wound to and from the ocean, unlike what the name implied, foot traffic became heavier, and my tension eased. Having grown up in Portland, being out alone at night still made my insides tighten, even though I'd come to learn how much the locals in Crystal Cove looked out for one another.

"Hi, Tabby!" a woman I knew from the café said as we passed her and her boyfriend.

"Hi!" I waved back. "This is my sister, Pepper. It's her first time in Crystal Cove."

Jolie introduced herself and her boyfriend to Pepper as we moved as a group toward a million twinkle lights, lighting up the sky down the beach. My witch friends had been chattering about the décor for the solstice festival all week, but I had to admit, I had no idea how much work they'd put into it until now, when it was all lit up.

Jeff and Jolie made conversation as we walked and as they found out Pepper was in medical school, Jeff, as a local nurse, found a lot to chat with her about.

Aside from lights, the witches also had vendor booths set up at every available space that was level enough to hold one. They'd even had a stretch of Shoreline Drive shut down for the night, and I was doubly glad that I hadn't chosen to bring my car.

"Wow, this looks really popular!" Pepper exclaimed.

In truth, most events in Crystal Cove were popular, even the ones held weekly. The locals were supportive of things like poetry readings and board game nights. Witchy Wednesday meetings in the café used to be just as popular, but in the last several months, it seemed the witches' bickering was putting them at odds with the rest of the community. I was glad to see so many locals and even some out-of-towners were filling up tonight's festival.

I tested Pepper's tolerance for magic talk with, "The witches have been planning this particular event for months. Should we find a booth for you to have your fortune told?"

She tilted her head at me, but before she could ask if I was serious, we arrived at the first vendor booth, manned by none other than the Queen Witch herself, Marigold Weathers.

Marigold was busy barking orders at one of the young men who worked at Happy Hardware to move a vendor booth that was sitting right in the middle of the road. I wondered why she cared, as the road was shut down for the night, but then she pointed up and said, "It's going to interfere with our performances!"

I had heard something about some of the witches performing, but I hadn't considered what that might involve until now. Jeff and Jolie moved along toward the festival, but this made me even more excited about showing the town off to my sister. She'd always loved theatrical performances. Even though Marigold seemed stressed in getting everything in order, I was disappointed I hadn't had a chance to introduce Pepper to her in the café, and couldn't help interrupting her flow when the young man took off to move the booth.

"Marigold? This is my sister, Pepper." When she stared at me and didn't respond, I added, "Remember how I told you she was coming to town for the solstice festival?"

Marigold gave a slight nod, but then rushed off toward the Town Hall, without a word of greeting. I pursed my lips as I watched her go. That was unlike Marigold Weathers. Even before she'd known and trusted me, she'd put up a friendly front.

I turned to Pepper. "Sorry. Marigold is in charge of the whole festival. I probably should have waited until it was underway to introduce you." I hesitated, but Marigold's comment in the café earlier was still bothering me, and so I hoped by talking about it, I might be able to relax a little more. "I also overheard talk in the café that Marigold has been receiving death threats, so she's probably extra stressed by that."

"Death threats? This town, Tabby. It's not what I imagined." Pepper watched Marigold's purple hair and flowy full-length orange dress as she rushed off. I thought again of the interaction we'd come upon with Frank and the man with the gambling problem at the marina. She wasn't getting a good introduction to Crystal Cove, was she? I immediately regretted telling Pepper about the death threat, especially when she raised an eyebrow after Marigold and asked, "She's one of your friends?"

It was difficult to explain my place with the witches. I felt a connection with the witches as a group because of my own affinity to magic, yet the fact that I couldn't openly talk about my own family brand of magic held me back from officially joining their group. It left me always feeling a little on the outskirts. I opened my mouth to try to delve into a little of the explanation of the local witches, but before I got a word out, Pepper's attention was diverted to another booth down the road.

"They have candy apples! Oh, Tabbichase, we have to get one!"

The last time Pepper and I had shared a candy apple was when we were kids. I remembered the specific time, because it had been at a campaign benefit our dad had been holding. We were always meant to be the perfect, well-behaved children at such events, so when we ended up with the candy coating all over our faces and clothes, and even in our hair, our dad had torn a strip off of us at home and made a new rule that we were forbidden from eating at any of his future political events.

As I followed Pepper to the booth, I saw the moment for what it was: Two women accepting their adulthood and ability to make their own choices. Pepper pointed to a caramel apple with nuts and marshmallows on the outside. Out of pure rebellion against my father, I asked for the messier red candy apple.

The witch who served us was Sheena Park, who I'd gotten to know fairly well. She was wearing her witch hat tonight. "Are you paying separately?" she asked, looking between us.

"Nope, I've got this!" I said, already holding out a twenty.

I waited for my change. When I turned back around with the two apples, Pepper was squatted down and looked as though she was whispering something to Sherlock.

I blinked, standing with my hands full and not knowing what to say. Could she hear Sherlock? Or was she so put off by the witch hat that she felt more comfortable with my cat? I felt confused for a second watching them.

Pepper started to laugh, which I thought made it clear she *could* hear Sherlock, but then she stood, took her apple from me, and said, "I was just thinking of that fundraiser where we both got candy apple all over ourselves!"

Huh. Maybe she wasn't conversing with my cat after all. And as we moved along the road and she veered away from a booth that promised tarot card readings, I realized if she could converse with my cat, chances were good she wouldn't be so automatically at ease with it.

A stage was set up over the rocky beach, near the water. Several people were perched on nearby rocks, as though waiting for a performance, and right then, our newly-elected Mayor Matthew Kelsey took to the stage to officially open the festival.

"Hello? Yes." He tapped the microphone a few times to make certain it was working. Mayor Kelsey had been renting his mansion to the local witches for their Halloween haunted house for several years, but I only knew him from the one campaign event he'd held in the café in early November before the election. I'd barely spoken to the man, but he had a good politician smile, much like our dad's. "I don't believe there was a permit issued for the road closure tonight," he said, "so please be wary of traffic on your way out. And I'll expect the roads to be fully functional by eight a.m. tomorrow."

With that, he left the stage. He shook hands with some nearby folks as he descended the stairs, looking happy enough, but it sure wasn't much of a festival opening.

Pepper and I waited for a few minutes, to see if anyone else would take the stage to provide a welcome or some entertainment, but it remained empty. With so many people around, I found my thoughts drifting from the shoreline to the stage to the vendor booths and back again, not sure what to do next. I must have been tired from the full week of both working at the café, and getting the houseboats ready for visitors.

Two hands caught me by surprise around my waist. I yelped and then turned to see Jay, grinning from ear to ear.

"You got the night off?" I asked my detective friend.

He looked between me and Pepper. I'd told him my sister was coming into town, but I was too caught off guard and excited to see him to immediately introduce them.

"In a sense." He raised an eyebrow. I'd known Detective Jay Jameson long enough to read this kind of body language and cryptic response. It meant he was on duty tonight, but undercover, a task made easier by his perpetually casual wardrobe. Tonight he looked extra attractive in jeans and a cream-colored sweater under his jacket. He extended a hand. "You must be Tabby's sister?"

"Pepper." She kept her hands in her pockets for a long time, but then seemed to clue in that he was waiting for a shake and pulled one hand out. Pepper and I didn't look alike. She had dark shiny hair, a lot like my mom's, while our brother Zach was blond after our dad. I was the only redhead in the family, the only person under five-six in the family, and the only one in the family who hadn't known who she was or what she wanted to become from the age of five. But as Pepper grinned at Jay and he looked between us, for the first time I felt like Pepper and I were more similar than I'd ever realized.

"Tabby was really excited that you could get down here for a visit. Do you know how long you're staying?"

Pepper glanced at me before answering. I had made plans for her to be here for the long weekend, and then I figured she'd want to get to our parents' house for the holidays. But she said, "I'm in no hurry to leave."

Jay nodded and touched my shoulder. "I'd better go and say hi to some others."

This was code for *I need to get an overview of the event and keep an eye on more than just you two.*

I smiled. "Will we see you later?"

Jay met my eyes. "Of course."

As he moved off, Marigold took to the stage, barking orders at young workers on her way until the second she touched the microphone, when she pasted on an enormous grin. Even though it was clearly fake, Marigold had the kind of charisma that still made others smile in response.

"Good evening, everybody! Thank you for coming. We, the witches of Crystal Cove, love your energy and our magic feeds off of it." Her booming voice brought a hush over the crowd. "So we begin the evening with the gift exchange ceremony. If you have a gift for someone, please exchange it with a friend. That generosity will stir up the powerful magic we need for our later events. And if you didn't bring any gifts, not to worry! There are plenty available at our vendor booths."

I chuckled under my breath. This was Marigold's not-so-sneaky way of making a profit tonight.

But the people of Crystal Cove were supportive folk. Whether or not they could read Marigold's underlying motives, most of them started to wander toward the dozen or so vendor booths, many of which held dream catchers and special stones and carvings.

I had spoken to Marigold and the other witches a dozen times in the café this week, and even I had not caught wind of this gift-giving ceremony, which was probably intentional.

"Let's go get each other something." Pepper's eyes lit up. She had always been a sucker for a gift. When we were kids, our parents could get her to clean practically the whole house for a dollar-store toy.

I had no doubt Marigold would be taking a large financial cut from everything sold tonight, and we likely wouldn't find much in the way of inexpensive trinkets, but my sister seemed so excited, and it was her first time in Crystal Cove. I wanted to erase the poor impression the town had given off so far, so I smiled and led the way back toward the booths.

Most of them were crowded by this point. When I spotted familiarity along the outskirts, I grabbed Pepper's arm and tugged her in that direction. "You have to meet my friend Rachael. She has a wonderful artistic talent."

Rachael's booth wasn't nearly as busy, probably because of its location, practically on the steps of the Town Hall and at the very edge of the festivities. I wondered if she and Marigold were fighting again. While the majority of the festival was lit by about a million white twinkle lights, the Town Hall was trimmed on every beam and window frame with multi-colored Christmas lights. There was even a large Christmas tree outside the main doors, which somehow seemed to contrast the festival.

"Tabby! This must be your sister?" Rachael called as we moved closer and her one customer moved onto another booth empty-handed.

I made the introductions and then told Rachael, "Can you do something fun with Pepper's name?"

Rachael constructed what she called "Word Art." Every piece was unique. She had done the lettering on the side of the *Lady of Fortune* earlier this year, and then a few months later created a different type of lettering, complete with whiskers and crystals, to make an art piece out of Sherlock's name. Of the pieces she had on display, the name Juliana was in a loopy writing with colorful daisies sprouting out from every serif, and the name Mark had a collaboration of intersecting roads with tiny cars driving on it.

"Of course!" Rachael said. As usual, she wore a short black dress with black-and-white striped tights peeking out the bottom. Tonight she also wore her witch's hat, which had been passed down from her grandmother. "I just need to know a little more about you.

What are your hobbies?" she asked Pepper.

Pepper looked to me with a blank expression.

I could help. "Pepper has been in medical school, or aiming toward medical school her whole life, but despite her dedication, she's still the most fun-loving person I know. She has an infectious laugh and makes everyone she's around feel at ease. She may not have a lot of hobbies, due to time constraints, but she's going to have the best bedside manner of any of the hospital staff, I promise you that."

Pepper blinked fast, like my words were making her tear up.

I lightened the mood by nudging her shoulder, and saying, "She also likes mice. Fake ones, not real ones," I added.

She pushed me back. "That was when I was, like, ten."

"So you don't still have eight million little critters in every crevice of your dorm room?"

"No." Her tone was righteous, until she murmured. "I had to pack up my dorm at the end of the semester."

Rachael smiled at our sisterly banter. "You know, it was your Aunt Lizzie who first started the gift-giving ceremonies in Crystal Cove? She was the one who made us see that generosity increased our magic." Rachael's face fell a little when she added, "Except now it's been turned into another way for us to make money."

It wasn't the first time I'd heard of Aunt Lizzie's drive to make the town a stronger community, and to try and make peace between witches and non-witches. My insides warmed at Rachael's statement, wondering if Pepper felt anything at all from her words. Pepper hadn't visited Aunt Lizzie nearly as much as me when we were kids. She'd hardly known our aunt.

I pulled out my wallet and passed Rachael a couple of twenties, but she held out a hand. "No, let this be my gift to both of you." I could tell she missed how things used to be when Aunt Lizzie was alive, and I wished in this moment that I had been able to be a part of the community back then.

"But, Rachael," I said. I knew she needed the money to supplement her housecleaning jobs.

However, she wouldn't have any of it. "Come back and collect your artwork in about an hour," she said with a grin that was all forced chin, like she wasn't going to let me argue this.

I thanked her, all while trying to think of a gift I could give her. Not only was she generous beyond her means, she'd just shown my sister the side of Crystal Cove I'd wanted her to see.

As we turned to walk away, another of the local witches, Donna, caught my eye. Donna was the most beautiful of all the witches, maybe even the most beautiful person I'd met in real life. But now she wore a deep scowl and was arguing with an equally good-looking man near an outer stairwell of the Town Hall.

I couldn't hear them from where I stood and turned back to Rachael. "Do you think everything's okay with Donna?" I motioned toward them.

Rachael sighed. "Oh, I'm sure they're fine. That's her boyfriend Nate Miller. We keep telling her she should break up with him, because they're always arguing, but she won't listen. She says he's a really good guy, just over-protective, which of course seems like the last type of person Donna should date."

Donna didn't normally dress loud like Marigold or witchy like Rachael, but tonight she wore a gold lamé jumpsuit.

She had started her own souvenir shop from scratch, and was in the midst of starting a local knitting club, and I'd always seen her as more business minded than flashy and emotional like many of the other local witches.

Her boyfriend Nate pointed up to a platform near the top of the metal staircase, and that was when I saw a wire that connected to our Town Hall. I followed it with my gaze and it went all the way to the lighthouse, a dozen yards out to sea on the wave-swept reef. My eyes widened with a sudden new thought.

"Wait, Donna's not doing some kind of high-wire act, is she?"

"Shhh!" Rachael moved closer and dropped to a whisper. "We're not supposed to call it that. We're not supposed to mention the wire."

No doubt this was a directive from Marigold. I looked between Donna and the wire, and crinkled my brow. Did

Marigold really think no one would see the wire, if no one mentioned it? I mean, I guess I might not have noticed if Nate hadn't pointed right at it, but if one of the witches was suddenly swinging from it, wouldn't everyone know?

I shook my head. Even though I hadn't been with my Aunt Lizzie since I was a child, she always made the magic of Crystal Cove seem so much more legit. Even I had experienced true magic since moving to Crystal Cove. Meanwhile, at every turn, Marigold seemed to be faking something to put on a show. It made me wonder if she had any true magical abilities at all.

"Don't worry, I'll keep an eye on Donna," Rachael told me, waving me toward the other booths. "Go enjoy yourselves."

At that moment, another couple wandered over to Rachael's booth, and as she turned away from us, I directed Pepper back toward the more populated booths.

She motioned to my sea glass necklace. "I don't want to seem ungrateful, but what I really want is one of those."

I touched my sea glass, which had remained consistently warm since my sister's arrival. "This? Oh, I made this one."

Her eyes lit up. "So you can make me one, too?"

I nodded, while inwardly torn. My sea glass had brought me strong intuition since I'd been wearing it. What if magical things started happening in Pepper's life as soon as she held a piece of sea glass in her hand. What would she think? Would it freak her out and send her running? Or would she embrace it quicker than I did and automatically be better at understanding the family gifting?

At the same time, I couldn't help but want to do whatever I could to make my sister happy. She had been through a hard six months, really struggling to get through her classes, and I knew she was ready for a break and to just enjoy her life for maybe the first time since she was a little kid.

We moved along to another vendor. Pepper was determined to find me a gift.

"I really don't need anything," I told her.

"I know you don't. That's not the point of a gift, though, is it?" She rolled her eyes and stopped at a booth that displayed about a million glimmering gemstones. The witch manning this booth was named Leanne, but I didn't know her beyond her first name.

"Are they real?" Pepper asked, but before Leanne could answer, Pepper had pulled a purple gemstone from its velvet pad and saw the price tag. "Five hundred dollars?" She looked to me. "Sorry, Tabbichase, I love you, but not quite enough for that."

"I wouldn't let you buy it for me anyway," I told her as we moved along to the next booth.

As we were between booths, Pepper stuffed her hands back into her pockets, frowned, and said, "I have this strange feeling, like something bad is going to happen."

I reached up to my sea glass, wondering if she could sense some intuition from it just from walking beside me. It was giving off a stronger warmth I hadn't noticed, and I had to wonder if she was right. I took a moment to gaze around the festival, but every person had a smile on his or her face.

I tried to shake the feeling as we shopped at three more booths, and finally Pepper found a hand-knit purple toque she bought me. It was overpriced too, at almost fifty dollars, but Pepper knew how much I loved purple and I didn't actually own a winter hat.

I wondered if these were from Donna's knitting club, or if perhaps these were all Donna's items, and the witch behind this booth was simply watching it for her. My thoughts were confirmed when I went to slip it on my head and saw the small tag boasting, "Designs by Donna."

I smiled, happy that we were supporting a witch friend, but then again wondered what kind of cut Marigold would take from the sale. By the time we left the vendor booth, a group of witches had taken the stage. At first glance, I thought they were doing some sort of dance, but as they tossed what looked to be a blue sparkly beach ball between them, it trailed glittery lights in the air. We moved closer so we could hear them chanting.

"Bring your gifts and light a trove, get it all in Crystal Cove," the dozen witches chanted from the stage.

"What are they doing?" Pepper asked me, as though I was the expert.

I didn't want to say it just looked like theatrics to me, so instead I told her, "They usually like to have some buildup for whatever big event they have planned." Again, I glanced up at the wire.

It was at least three stories up above the festival and continued over the ocean toward the lighthouse. The thought of someone I knew hanging from it up so high gave me a shiver and I pulled on my new purple hat. At the same time, I was curious to see how they expected her flight to look anything other than acrobatic.

The stage was now almost completely filled with lit up sparkles. I supposed most people at this festival were more than willing to see magic pretty much everywhere they looked.

After the glitter ball toss, Marigold took the stage and thanked at least thirty sponsors for the event. I was surprised so many people and businesses had trusted her with the funds, after the way she'd recently ripped off a tourist of a lot of money. Part of me wondered if that was why Jay was working the festival tonight—to make sure she wasn't taking financial advantage of anyone in the town. I wondered if he'd had a close look at that gemstones booth.

I was lost in thought until Marigold announced the Flight of the Witch of Crystal Cove. "As you know, I've been honored to serve as Queen Witch over most of the last year, but as I'm moving on in years, I'm happy to introduce our new Queen this evening." She motioned toward the Town Hall, where Donna was climbing onto nothing other than...a broomstick. Sheena Park and another witch I didn't know were assisting her, and from our distance, it looked as though they were lifting her up into the air with no assistance.

Having seen the wire earlier, I had to assume the broomstick was attached on either end. I couldn't help my analytical brain from kicking in to figure out exactly how they'd made this work and how safe it might be.

I wondered if I was the only one who noticed there wasn't any actual magic involved. I couldn't get over the irony that the event that was driving the excitement at this magic solstice festival didn't even involve any magic. People had left the fortune-telling and tarot card reading booths to see this fancy orchestrated trick.

Even though Donna looked nervous from a distance, she was one of those really capable people. She wasn't normally much of a risk taker. Perhaps it was her boyfriend Nate who had put fearful thoughts in her head.

But then, quite suddenly, my sister started whispering, "I don't like this, I don't like this at all," almost too quietly to hear.

I held my breath as Donna took off and sailed overhead. Trying to keep myself calm, I kept my eyes on the Town Hall, wondering if anyone else was up there to perform the trick after Donna.

But no one appeared, and a sudden shriek made me swing around in the other direction toward the lighthouse.

Donna was no longer on the wire.

Not only that, but the wire sprang toward the crowd like a crazed windsock, but a hundred times as dangerous. People ducked in every direction, and screams and shouts erupted from all around the crowd.

"Watch out!"

"Duck!"

"Get out of the way!"

"Call an ambulance," someone yelled, which meant the wire must have struck someone.

I looked toward the lighthouse, and then below the lighthouse in horror. Because Donna's body was splayed on the rocks of the reef, and she wasn't moving.

Chapter Three

As I FOUGHT MY way through the crowd with Pepper on my heels, all I could think of was how glad I was that I hadn't seen Donna fall. I didn't want that image in my head. As my sea glass turned to ice around my neck, my gut clenched. Donna still wasn't moving, but a small motorboat pulled up along the reef right where she had fallen.

The person on the boat wore dark clothes and with his back to me, I couldn't make out his face, but I wondered if it was her boyfriend, Nate Miller.

By the time I made it to the edge of the water, my other detective friend, Aaron Thom had boarded a small rowboat with another officer and headed out toward the reef. As he rowed, he yelled something toward the man on the reef, but with his voice aimed the other direction, I couldn't make out any of his words. Meanwhile, Jay was at the shoreline, keeping the crowd back and trying to calm them down.

Aaron stepped out of the rowboat onto the reef and while his officer friend tied up the boat, he rushed over to check on Donna and the other figure stepped aside.

"Is she... is she okay?" I asked, swallowing down my emotions so I wouldn't force Jay to deal with me as a bumbling mess, on top of everything else he had to deal with tonight.

"We don't know yet." His voice was gentle, but then it took on its authoritative boom as he said, "Please step back up toward the road," to all the people who were trying to get as close as possible to Donna to see what had happened. Even though the wire now hung limp in the middle of the festival, people gave it a wide berth as they moved back, as though it may suddenly spring to life again. Jay called, "Gather the people you came with and exit via the main road. If you're hurt, stay where you are, we will have medical personnel arriving momentarily."

"Can I help anyone?" Pepper's gaze darted around the moving crowd. "I have medical training."

I had told Jay about Pepper's schooling, but she wasn't licensed to practice yet. She could help as a layperson, but would never want to go beyond the direction of the local authorities.

"Please," Jay told her. "Find out if there are any serious injuries in the crowd, so we can get to them as soon as our paramedics arrive."

Pepper rushed off and he pulled out his phone, which had been lit up by a new message. As the beam from the lighthouse landed on him, I could see that Aaron also had his phone in his hands. He was texting Jay with an update.

When Jay looked up from his phone, his countenance appeared momentarily shocked, then a second later broken. He cleared his throat to recover.

"Listen, Tabby. It's probably best that you head home for the night. We're going to have to shut down the festival in order to get the medical examiner to the reef without a lot of upset."

I nodded, but my adrenaline had kicked in in the last thirty seconds and I had no intention of leaving. Maybe it was because of my sister's example, but I felt ultra-focused on any way I might be able to assist. "Let me help, Jay. Tell me what to do." I momentarily wondered if we should get Pepper over to the reef to help Donna. She was right here, after all. Then again, if there was any hope at all for Donna, there would be much more panic behind Jay's words.

Jay told me, "There's a stack of pylons up by the Town Hall. If you could form a perimeter line and help direct people away from the festival, without blocking the road—"

"I'm on it," I said.

He explained more, but I was already in motion. "It would be really helpful if the emergency vehicles could get through quickly. Also, can you call Frank at the marina? Tell him what's happened and ask if he could get a boat over here for us to use?"

"You bet," I called back as he picked up his phone to talk to Aaron.

As I hurried past Pepper, on her knees helping a woman who appeared to have fallen in the panic from the wild wire, I slowed. Pepper sounded perfectly calm, comforting the woman, and I knew she'd make a great doctor one day, even if her aim was to become a research doctor more than working with patients. On the other hand, I was struck incapacitated once again, just watching the stress of it all on this woman.

It was all I could do to remember what Jay had tasked me with and force my feet one after another toward the main road. As I walked, I looked for serious injuries, but thankfully, so far, I hadn't seen anyone who had been actually struck by the wire. I navigated to the contacts on my phone and dialed Frank.

While I told Frank what had happened, I located the pylons and did exactly what Jay had asked. Every three seconds, someone asked me if Donna was okay and I had to explain that we didn't have any details on the accident yet, but the best way they could help was to clear their party out of the area as quickly and as safely as possible.

On my way back to help Pepper, Marigold stepped into my path. "What are they doing to find out who did this?" she demanded.

"Who did this?" I held out my hands to her. "To Donna?" What was she saying?

She nodded her head fervently. "I've been receiving those death threats all week, and then this happens? You have to be able to see the correlation!"

I had to admit, when Marigold had mentioned the death threats, part of me had thought she'd been making them up, in order to get attention. She hadn't seemed worried thirty seconds after she mentioned them. But now, what I saw on her face was pure concern.

"Marigold," I said, using my most consoling voice. "I really don't think one thing has to do with the other. It's devastating, but with dangerous stunts like this one, accidents do happen—"

She shook her head, almost violently. "This was not an accident! I made absolutely certain of that!"

I pulled back, wondering if her crazed tone was simply the case of guilt. Marigold had likely convinced Donna to perform the stunt. "How could you know that?" My voice still oozed compassion, even though I was feeling less and less for her in the moment, and more for Donna's friends and family.

"Because we practiced! Multiple times!" She flailed her hands. "Plus there was a safe wire, just in case."

I put a hand on her shoulder. "Be sure to tell Detective Jameson the details of your practice runs and the apparatus." I was no physics expert, but my immediate thought was that if two wires couldn't bear the strain of the weight of a grown woman, the sudden pressure on a single wire would quickly snap that one, too. It may have seemed like they'd snapped at the same time, but they probably hadn't.

Marigold strode for Jay.

Twenty minutes later, when most of the crowd had been cleared out, I found Pepper standing near two paramedics at an ambulance.

"Was anyone seriously hurt?" I asked when I was still a few feet away. One paramedic automatically looked to the reef, where medics and police officers surrounded Donna. "Anyone here ashore?" I added.

Pepper shook her head. "Just scrapes and bruises. A lot of people were really shaken up by the events, though."

No doubt. I still felt shaken up by it and as I neared the ambulance, exhaustion overtook me. "I should probably... I should get you back to the boat."

Pepper offered a wry smile. "Still trying to protect me, sis? Why don't we ask your detective friend if we can do anything else before we go?"

I would have done that anyway, but I didn't tell Pepper that, because part of me was trying to protect her, and not just from seeing a dead body. Given her medical training, she would probably deal with that a lot better than I would. I was more concerned with what kind of magical implications another death of a witch in town might have. For all I knew, the reason why my aunt's magic had so strongly accosted me when I came to town was because there was a dead witch at that point, too.

This time it was much more painful, though, because I had considered Donna Davine a friend. She would never come into the café again, never chat with me at the counter while she waited for me to brew her tea, never set up her knitting needles on the back tables.

The paramedics thanked Pepper for her help, but I felt like I barely had enough brainpower left to get us home.

"You okay?" She took my arm and led us toward the rocky shore. Since we'd left Jay, another ambulance as well as the car of the medical examiner, Mick Short, had parked as close as they could get to the water, and Jay was in the midst of sending Frank across the water, loaded up with more emergency workers and their supplies.

I didn't want to interrupt, but I also didn't want to answer Pepper's question, as I really wasn't feeling okay at the moment. I forged ahead.

As Jay pushed the large rowboat off, toward the reef, I took a step away from Pepper and moved in behind him. He turned back around. "Oh, Tabby?"

"We've cleared out most of the crowd. I assured the witches you'd have some sort of security overnight, to keep an eye on the vendor booths?" I'd do it myself, if he didn't have the manpower, but having the witches come back in to pack everything up would take hours.

Jay nodded. "At this rate, my whole staff will probably be here through the night. It certainly won't make things easy to investigate with the body out on the reef."

I swallowed at him referring to Donna as "the body." He normally watched his words more, but he'd grown comfortable with me helping with investigations and often spoke to me as candidly as he did the other officers on the force.

"So there's an investigation?" Pepper asked, her voice filled with worry. I wondered if she had overheard Marigold's concerns.

"An investigation is always required in the case of a public death of this kind," I answered my sister, having learned this from the few investigations I'd been involved with. It would likely be something she'd learn as she got closer to her medical degree. But then, because I'd promised Marigold, I turned back to Jay. "Did Marigold speak to you? She's convinced of some foul play with Donna's fall. She feels the witches have too many enemies, and that there had been a fail-safe wire rigged so nothing like this could happen."

Jay nodded. "Yes, she explained that. Our forensics team is currently looking into the engineering of the apparatus." He motioned to the reef. "Any other reason Marigold suspected someone would have done this on purpose?"

I still didn't see that this was necessarily tied in, but I told him anyway. "She says the witches are always facing opposition in Crystal Cove, but the latest stress was some death threats she had been receiving."

Jay's head snapped up from where he'd been making notes. "Donna had been receiving death threats?"

"No, no. Not her," I told him quickly. My brain was too tired to watch my wording. "Marigold had been receiving them, just this last week." I shook my head. "I don't see how they're tied in, either, but Marigold is more stressed than I've ever seen her, and she really believes there's something wrong here."

Jay nodded slowly. "Why don't you offer to take her home, check out those death threats, and see if there's anything that could be tied to this. Ask Marigold if you can take the death threats with you for our investigation, or if not, snap some photos of them for the time being."

I nodded in agreement with everything he told me, repeating his instructions over and over in my head so I wouldn't forget them. When he had to answer another call from Aaron, I headed off without interrupting him to say goodbye.

"Is that detective really asking for our help?" Pepper asked as she practically had to jog to catch up.

I chuckled under my breath, because he wasn't asking for Pepper's help, exactly. "It's a pretty small police force here in town. I help out when I can."

"Wait." She stopped in place before we made it to Marigold. "Where's your cat? Where's Sherlock?"

I hadn't thought about him all night, but if there was an investigation of any kind in the works, I had no doubt he was sniffing around doing his own sleuthing.

I surveyed the vendor area, which was now lit by some bright standing lights, brought in by police officers. Several officers now had little to do, as they couldn't get to the reef at the moment, and I had already done their job in clearing away the crowd.

Finally, I spotted movement over near the Town Hall. "Wait, I think I see him."

I marched off quickly, not expecting Pepper to follow, but she was right on my heels.

"So are you saying this sort of thing is normal? You helping the local police with their investigations?"

I thought I had alluded to this enough in our recent phone calls that she wouldn't be quite so shocked. I didn't want it getting back to Mom that I was in any kind of danger, so I told her a half-truth. "Sometimes I help with tangential details. Don't worry, Pepps. They're not in any hurry to put me in the line of fire."

"And what are you up to, Sherlock the investigator?" she asked my cat as soon as we got close to him near the outer stairwell of the Town Hall. The stairwell had been cordoned off with bright yellow police tape.

Even though she asked it jokingly, Sherlock was busy sniffing at a cold drink cup sitting on the ground near the base of the stairs. It looked like any other fast-food drink cup that would have been sold at any other fair. The difference was... a memory immediately hit me, upon seeing the cup. Hadn't Donna Davine's boyfriend been holding a cup like that one when they'd been arguing less than an hour ago? When she'd still been alive.

What if they hadn't been arguing because he'd been overprotective and concerned about her stunt? What if they'd been arguing about something completely different?

That idea, combined with Marigold's concern about possible foul play made my mind quickly ricochet to murderous possibilities. While Pepper bent down and cooed over my cat, I shot off a quick text to Jay.

What do you know about a guy named Nate Miller? Apparently, he'd been dating Donna, and I saw them arguing at the base of the Town Hall about

an hour ago. He left his drink cup behind, which probably still has his fingerprints on it.

Jay was now surrounded by police officers, all wanting to do something to help. When my text came through, he pulled his phone out to read it. Then he looked up my way. I pointed down to the drink container. He nodded and said something to a nearby officer. Then he gave me one more solid nod, which I knew meant thank you and turned back to the other officers to get back to business.

While it was always difficult to leave the scene of a death while it was being investigated, I'd come to learn that this wasn't my time to be of the most help. In the immediate aftermath of something like this, all the police in town would swarm the area and investigate every detail in the best way they knew how. If I stayed, I'd only be in the way.

As if to punctuate this fact, Officer Grant made his way toward me and cleared his throat, in a directive to step away from the evidence.

I suppressed an eye roll. He had plenty enough room to retrieve the drink cup, and it wasn't as if I didn't know better than to touch the thing. But I moved away just the same.

No, in the midst of this bustling investigation was not my time to help.

Besides, I'd been working with Jay for long enough that I felt quite sure he'd be by the *Lady of Fortune* first thing in the morning to discuss the case with me. For the moment, he'd given me another job to do.

"Do you want to take Sherlock back to the boat?" I asked Pepper, my eyes focused on Marigold.

But she let out a balk and Sherlock's words came loud and clear into my head.

Can't leave me behind! Interview purple witch.

Right, so it was the three of us then.

"Alright. Let's go see what this purple witch has to tell us about her death threats."

Chapter Four

MARIGOLD ASSURED ME OVER and over again that she was fine to drive, so I ended up getting my own car and then meeting her back at her place. She'd still seemed really jumpy and upset, but when I told her I wanted to have a look at her death threats and pass them along to Jay, she met my eyes, grabbed my hands, and thanked me for taking this seriously.

And yet when Pepper, Sherlock, and I arrived at her basement door, she looked down at my cat and let out a frustrated sigh.

"I can't..." She shook her head. "Some of my clients have allergies, you know?"

Her basement was where Marigold brought her fortune-telling clients, along with anyone else who came to visit. I had never been in her upstairs, but had glimpsed it once and been surprised by the plainness of it. I could have suggested we go upstairs if it was her clients she was concerned with, but I had a strong feeling the answer would still be no. Marigold didn't like cats, or at least she didn't like *my* cat.

For the first time, I wondered if she could sense the magic in Sherlock. Then again, wouldn't that make her want to keep Sherlock closer?

All these thoughts passed through my mind in less than a couple of seconds, and instead I decided on saying, "That's fine. Sherlock can wait outside."

Sherlock heard and understood my words, and without hesitation, wandered off toward Marigold's dormant azalea bushes, giving them a sniff, as though they might provide a clue.

I had no doubt, as we moved into her basement, that the instant we were out of sight, Sherlock would find other much more interesting places around here to investigate.

I'd been in Marigold's basement several times, but this was all brand new for Pepper. She stared around at the dream catchers and knickknacks, statues and incense sticks. The place smelled strongly of sage. I'd heard people burned sage to help cleanse negative energy, and I wondered if that had been the case here.

There were only two seats on either side of the small table in the middle of Marigold's one-room basement, and so I offered one to Pepper, assuming Marigold would take the other.

But she said, "I'll just go and get the death threats." It seemed odd, as she'd just come from upstairs, and now that seemed to be where she was returning. Why hadn't she brought them down with her in the first place? She knew we were coming and the purpose for our visit. On her way out, she lay the orange wrap she'd been wearing over a storage bin filled with what looked like a large spool of rope near the stairway.

"Does she really charge money to tell people's fortunes in here?" Pepper whispered. She'd seen the signage out front, and I had explained a little more about the town's Queen Witch on our way over.

I nodded. Marigold had recently lost some favor within the town when she'd taken financial advantage of an out-of-towner in mourning. Word got out, and when she was regularly getting snubbed around town, she had decided to give what was left of the money back to the mourning woman. Unfortunately, it hadn't raised people's trust in her any and I'd seen her working more and more hours at her son's grocery mart in town recently.

From Marigold's announcement at the festival, it was clear even she knew that Crystal Cove was ready for a new Queen Witch. I was just sad to know it would never be Donna.

I stayed to the outskirts of the basement, waiting for Marigold and thinking about this as though I was looking closer at her magic wares. I wondered if she had been pushing for Donna to be Queen Witch mainly so she could continue to manipulate the local witches through her. For some reason, I could concentrate a lot better here, and I had to wonder if some of her statues or carvings truly were infused with magic.

Thoughts of the tensions with Marigold gave me pause, and I wondered if she was worried that the town would blame her for Donna's accidental death. Perhaps that was why she was so determined to get the police suspecting foul play.

When Marigold descended the stairs, she held what looked like large index cards in her hands. She laid all four of them out on her small table, and I stood over Pepper's shoulder to look at them.

I had to blink a few times to clear my head, because before I even read any of the words, my immediate impression was that they looked like miniature versions of Rachael's word art. Pepper didn't hesitate to confirm this.

"Hey, these look similar to those art pieces that your friend was making. We never did get back there to pick up the one you had made for me." Pepper's words were casual, but as I read the clear threats, I held my breath, because if even Pepper saw the similarity, what did that mean for Rachael?

People like you are ruining Crystal Cove. This needs to end. YOU need to end.

Take out the Queen Bee and the workers will scatter.

Watch your back. It'll happen when you least expect it.

I won't rest until you drop dead, Marigold Weathers.

I read them all three times, then I took photos and made notes in my phone, so I wouldn't lose track of any of my immediate impressions. They were clearly directed at Marigold herself. But Marigold hadn't been the person to die. The person threatening seemed to focus on how Marigold was bringing down the town. And for some reason, he or she was trying to make it look like Rachael's handiwork.

As if she truly could read my mind, Marigold scoffed and waved a hand. "Well, Rachael would never do this. I'll tell you that much."

"No?" Pepper asked, honestly. She would make a good investigator, the way she asked open-ended questions and then sat back to wait for an answer. I was always tempted to jump in with a jumble of words when the silence became uncomfortable.

"Of course not." Marigold sat across from Pepper. "You see these jagged edges on the letters? Rachael paid a lot of money for her paint pens so they wouldn't do that. Besides, Rachael would never betray one of the local witches."

Even though I wholeheartedly agreed, it was nice to hear someone else say it. "But someone clearly wanted to shift the blame toward Rachael. Why do you think that is?"

Marigold let out a huff of a breath. "I have no idea."

That wasn't very helpful. "What leads you to believe these threats have anything to do with Donna's death?"

She pointed at different words such as *Crystal Cove* and *workers* and *scatter* as she spoke. "Someone clearly has an agenda against the witches in town. For all we know, that's why they're trying to make it look as though Rachael might want to kill me! Maybe they thought I'd be the one flying out to sea tonight. Whoever it is, they're trying to cause division, and how do we even know they'll stop with Donna? Maybe they aim to kill all of us!"

"Can I take these to Detective Jameson?" I asked.

She looked at me for a long moment. "I suppose, if you think they will help."

I expected that Marigold's fingerprints were all over the cardstock by now, hiding any prints of a possible suspect, but regardless, I asked her if she had a spare plastic bag. When she brought me one, I turned it inside out, to pick up the cards with the bag and sequestered them without actually touching them. While I did this, Pepper went to look out the window to check on Sherlock.

When the sudden thought came to me, I asked, "Hey, what do you know about Donna's boyfriend, Nate Miller?"

Marigold shrugged and stood, striding for the door as though she was hurrying us out now. "Not much. They hadn't been dating long." Her eyes widened. "Why? Do you think he was responsible?"

I wasn't about to fuel this fire. "I'm not saying that. We need a fuller picture of everyone who knew Donna or may have had a deadly motive—if what you say is correct and it wasn't an accident."

"Oh, it definitely was not an accident," Marigold told me, opening the door to let us out. She sounded confident for someone who really didn't have any proof. "But I know you'll help get to the bottom of this, Tabby. You and Detective Jameson."

As I left, I couldn't shake the glow of pride that came over me, even as I still had a clear sense that Marigold was only trying to carefully direct my next steps.

Chapter Five

ON THE WAY BACK to my car, we found Sherlock outside, sniffing around Marigold's big brown sedan.

"What is it, Sherlock?" I asked out loud before I remembered Pepper was with me and she would likely notice the oddity in it.

Sherlock knew better than to answer me in front of Pepper. He took one final sniff up at the car, and then turned to head for my Honda.

I texted Jay as I followed.

I got the death threats. Should I bring them by the festival area? Are you still there?

By the time we reached my car, I had gotten a reply.

Probably better if I come by tomorrow morning to get them. It's pretty crazy around here.

Crazy didn't deter me, as Jay had probably imagined it would. In fact, it made me itch to go there right this second. But I'd been learning to quell my eagerness and heed Jay's instructions. He was the skilled detective, after all, and more than anything, I didn't want to get in his way.

As if to push the matter, Pepper said, "Are we going back to the festival to give your detective friend those death threats?"

I put my car in gear and shook my head as I drove us back to the marina. "He said it's not a good time to come by.

He'll drop by and pick them up tomorrow sometime."

Pepper nodded, and she was more easily able to let the whole thing go. "I'm starving. Do you have food on the boat or should we pick something up?"

Not being from here, Pepper didn't realize that pretty much all of the local businesses had shut down to attend the festival. Even Olivia had planned to close the coffee shop by eight—and she was the most die-hard of the local business owners. I had planned to get us more than just candy apples at the festival, but we'd been so busy I hadn't gotten around to it.

"There's one place a few miles out of town that might be open," I told her. Even though I had food back at the boat, I couldn't seem to make my mind come up with anything I had the energy to cook tonight. Her suggestion of picking something up was all I could think about.

Thankfully Barney's, a burger place a few miles out of town, was indeed open.

"You stay here with Sherlock. I'll be right back," I told her. She must have been equally exhausted, because she didn't argue with me, and rather than focusing on my cat, she sat back and closed her eyes.

After ordering two cheeseburgers with fries and sodas at the counter, I stood near an empty table to check my phone while waiting for the food. There wasn't anything new from Jay, but I looked over the notes I'd made at Marigold's and suddenly felt energized with new ideas.

When I got back to the car, I passed Pepper the food and said, "I want to see if my friend Rachael is still up. She doesn't live too far from here. I know you're tired, but I promise, I won't be long."

Pepper seemed more concerned about her grumbling tummy than anything I had to say, so I drove straight to

Rachael's neighborhood. While waiting for my food, I'd made a note of some of my questions for her, and now I was glad, because as I pulled into a parking spot below Rachel's upper apartment suite, I could barely remember why I was here.

"Do you want your burger?" Pepper asked as I reached for the door.

I snagged a few fries from her open container, deciding that would have to hold me over. Exhaustion was overtaking me again, but I couldn't shake the feeling it was important to stop here. My warm sea glass was confirming it as I got closer to Rachael's apartment, saw the light on, and knocked.

"Oh? Tabby? What are you doing here?" Rachael was already in her long sleep T-shirt. It was always odd to see her out of her black-and-white striped tights, and somehow it made her look a few years younger than she was—like she could still be in high school with Katie. Her eyes were red from crying.

"Can I come in for a minute?" I asked.

Noticing the seriousness on my face, Rachael didn't hesitate to swing the door open wider.

"She's dead, isn't she?" Rachael asked. Her eyes brimmed with new tears.

I nodded and pulled her into a hug. Rachael sobbed for several long minutes, and I was glad I was here when she found out for sure. Rachael and Donna hadn't been close, exactly, but Rachael cared for all of the local witches as though they were her family.

When she finally pulled away, I proceeded with my first question for her. "Rachael, had you heard anything about Marigold receiving death threats lately?" I didn't need my notes in my phone. As though in response to Rachael's strong emotion, my mind had become ultra-focused. I didn't want to upset her any more than I already had, but I needed to get down to business.

She looked stunned by my question for a second, but then shook it off, and said, "Yes, she's been telling everybody. Why?"

"Has she shown you any of them?"

She nibbled her lip, probably surprised I was talking about anything other than Donna, but at the same time, I didn't think either of us really wanted to talk about Donna at the moment. "No. I don't think she's shown them to anybody."

Thankfully, Rachael was used to me asking questions she didn't always understand. She knew I helped Jay with investigations from time to time, and she knew I often couldn't share details. So she didn't usually push for extra information, but because this was regarding one of the witches, tonight she did.

"Why? Do you think she's making them up?"

I shook my head. "I've seen them. They're real." Before Rachael could react to this, I asked, "Is there any reason you can think of that someone would want to start problems between you and Marigold?"

She pulled back. "Me? No. I've been nothing but helpful to Marigold with setting up the solstice festival."

"You didn't have the most desirable location for your booth at the festival," I observed.

She shook her head. "I offered to take the spot near the Town Hall. Marigold was super stressed about where she was going to put all the vendors." This sounded like Rachael, always putting everybody else first. "What about the death threats, though?"

I knew for a fact Rachael had not sent the death threats to Marigold. As the real ones were in my car, I pulled the photos up on my phone and passed it over for her. I still felt a little like I might be overstepping on police procedures, but my warm sea glass confirmed this was the right thing. "Have a look. There are four of them."

Rachael flipped through the photos, zooming in and studying each one. I could tell by the dance of her eyebrows she had never seen them before and what was written was all new to her.

It was a couple of long minutes before she finally looked back at me, her brow furrowed. "Why do these look like my Word Art?"

I shrugged, taking my phone back. "That's what I hoped you could tell me." Worry covered her face, and she opened her mouth to say something, but I intercepted her words. "We know you didn't send them. I know it, and Marigold knows it. Marigold pointed out how your pens would never feather along the edges the way the ones on the death threats did."

This seemed to put Rachael's mind at ease. "But does someone want it to look like I'd sent them to Marigold?" She looked confused.

"It looks that way," I told her.

She didn't have any answers for me, and finally I figured I should get Pepper back to get some sleep. "Just call me if you think of anything that might be important," I said on my way out the door.

Thankfully, she hadn't asked if this could somehow be related to Donna's death. I didn't think it did, but I still felt a hesitation about giving a solid answer about that.

When we got back to the *Lady of Fortune*, while Pepper washed up in the bathroom, I headed to my aunt's bedroom to get into my pajamas. Sherlock waited until this moment to use his mind-speak from the middle of Aunt Lizzie's bed.

Magic sister going to help with mystery?

"Magic sister?" I asked in a whisper. "Are you saying Pepper has magical abilities?" I swallowed the note of jealousy that automatically poked at me.

Only with the crystal she's family magic.

Sherlock's words often didn't come out in flawless English, and who could blame him? He was a cat, for goodness sake! But I tried to navigate his words and make sense of them. "She has the family gift?" I whispered. "But what do you mean about the crystal?" I eyed my aunt's closet. I'd been certain to keep the one blue crystal I owned stashed away deep in the back of the closet so it wouldn't cause erratic thoughts in me. Seconds later, I dug through my pile of sweaters to the bottom, where I kept the crystal in a small jewelry box.

I sucked in a breath, opened the box...and the crystal was gone.

"Did she take it?" I asked Sherlock, turning back to the bed. "Did she have it with her at the festival tonight?"

But my cat was gone.

If Pepper had brought the crystal, it would explain why I'd had trouble concentrating through much of the evening when she was near. It also might explain why she'd had her hands jammed in her pockets all night.

Another sickening thought hit me: I barely knew how to wield the magic of the blue crystal, as it always seemed much too strong for me. What if Pepper had brought it to the festival and *made* the accident happen to Donna?

What if Marigold was correct, and there was foul play involved in Donna's death—but what if it wasn't *intentional* foul play?

Chapter Six

I HADN'T THOUGHT OF a way to broach the subject of the crystal with Pepper, but the next morning, I was up early thinking about it again. If I knew my sister, after the burger and fries last night, she'd have a carb hangover that would keep her in bed until noon.

My phone rang, and I answered, keeping my voice quiet. It was Rachael, and she immediately started talking.

"I need to ask around to the other witches. Someone has to know something about why anyone would try to make it look like I would send death threats!"

I wondered if she'd been up all night thinking about this, and suddenly felt guilty about bringing it up when she'd been ready for bed last night. "Let me talk to Jay this morning," I told her. "I'm hoping to show him the actual cards with the death threats when I get a minute with him. Let me see if he has any other thoughts before you go asking around." These were *death threats*, after all. I didn't want Rachael getting herself into any kind of danger by asking too many questions. "I'm going to call him right now. Don't do anything until you hear from me."

It took me a few minutes to get her to calm down, but finally she agreed and we hung up. Before I could pick up my phone again to dial Jay, there was a quiet knock at the door. When I opened it, Jay stood on the other side, looking haggard, as if he, too, had been up all night.

I motioned to the front deck, which was on the opposite end of the boat from where Pepper was sleeping.

"Let's talk out here," I said. "I'll grab us some coffee."

Jay nodded and slunk into one of my wrought-iron chairs on the deck. By the time I returned with a coffee for each of us, plus a couple of leftover scones I'd brought home from the café the afternoon before, Sherlock had helped himself to the chair across from Jay. They were staring intently at one another.

I truly wished there was some way to comprehend exactly who could communicate with my cat and who could not. It was one of the questions I asked Sherlock regularly, but he either didn't understand the question or chose not to answer.

I set the coffee and scones down and then grabbed for the plastic bag full of death threats from under my arm and placed that in front of him. He retrieved a pair of latex gloves from his briefcase and then opened the bag, studying each card one by one.

"You haven't touched these?"

I shook my head. "But Marigold was handling them pretty freely, so I'm sure they're full of her prints."

Jay nodded. As he paused on the one that promised that the writer would see Marigold Weathers dead, it occurred to me that he wouldn't be studying them so thoroughly if he didn't think they could somehow be connected to the tragedy from the night before.

"Wait, did you find something from last night? Did it look as though there was foul play involved in Donna's death?"

Jay took in a big breath and let it out slowly. Then he slid the death threats back into the bag. "Unfortunately, yes. It seems that the wire cable used for the stunt showed signs of being severed with some sort of cable cutters."

My eyes widened. "Someone truly killed Donna?" My question came out in a whisper.

Jay nodded solemnly. He knew Donna about as well as I did. None of us were close, but Donna was a presence in Crystal Cove. The town wouldn't be the same without her.

"I'll get forensics to look at the death threats, to see if they could be related."

In our previous investigations, I'd learned that it was better to be completely upfront with Jay than to hold anything back. Unfortunately, the parameters of my family magical gift dictated that I physically was unable to share about our gifting with anyone outside the family. I'd tried many times to fill Jay in on both my magic and Sherlock's, only to find the words getting stuck in my throat. But I could tell him this: "The death threats definitely bear a resemblance to Rachael Adams's Word Art, but even Marigold could recognize that the jagged edges don't match with Rachael's expensive paint pens."

Jay took a sip of coffee and then twisted his lips. "But perhaps someone wanted it to look as though Rachael had sent them."

"Rachael wants to look into it. She wants to ask questions around her witch friends." I bowed my head to hide the guilt on my face. "I went to see her last night, to see if she had any idea who might want to cause division between her and Marigold."

When I peeked up, Jay was nodding and writing, looking unbothered. "Did she have any suggestions of who might be behind the threats?"

I shook my head. "But if this could tie into Donna's death, I'm afraid for her, being out there and asking questions."

Jay took in a big breath and let it out slowly. "I agree. Let me text Aaron and see if he can spare an officer to stick with her while we figure this out."

That made me feel a lot better. "I'd had the thought that Marigold might have sent them to herself for extra attention." Jay's gaze snapped up to meet mine, but I quickly added, "After last night, though, and seeing how shaken up she was, I don't really believe that anymore."

Jay pulled out a notepad and jotted something down. I wasn't happy that I'd thrown Marigold into the ring of possible suspects, but at the same time, Marigold had done enough underhanded things in the nine months I'd known her that I figured it wouldn't hurt her to have to prove her innocence.

As Sherlock rubbed against my shins, though, it reminded me of how interested he'd been in Marigold's car the night before. On that note, I asked, "What would it take to get a search warrant to look through her house and her car?"

Jay shrugged. "We'd have to have strong probable cause of guilt. Why? What are you thinking we'd find?"

I honestly had no idea. I shook my head. "Sherlock was sniffing around her car. That's all." I'd been looking for ways to gradually indicate to Jay that my cat had some sort of magical insight into the world without actually coming up against the family-magic rules and saying it. At least Jay was open to magic of all kinds, and I suspected he would catch on.

Sure enough, he made another note, nodding. He drained the last of his coffee in one gulp and picked up a scone and a napkin, as if to take it with him. "Are you available to come back to the festival grounds with me?"

"You bet!" I looked down and remembered I was still in my pajamas. "Just give me two minutes."

He bit into his scone, chewed, and said, "And let's bring Sherlock."

Chapter Seven

I GRABBED A SWEATER and a pair of jeans from where I'd stowed some of my clothes in the front closet and hurried into the boat's bathroom to change. When I emerged, I scribbled a note for my sister.

Pepper,

Just gone for a walk with Jay. I shouldn't be long. Text me when you're awake.

Tabby

I hoped by keeping it casual, she might interpret it to be a friendly walk and not an investigative one, which might spur her on to come and find us. I hadn't had a chance to think more about whether or not Pepper had taken the blue crystal from my closet and what that might mean if she did. I'd also had another thought last night as I was falling asleep. The *Lady of Fortune* had its own magic going on. More than once it had provided dresses in my closet or fresh pastries in my kitchen, and it even provided a new dress for Pepper last night. Who was to say the boat wasn't responsible for taking my one blue crystal from the closet and swallowing it up?

And if that was the case, would I ever get it back?

As Jay and I walked toward the festival grounds, he gave me a rundown of what had been discovered the night before.

"The wire was severed on the reef side, so it had to have been done by someone who was already over there."

"It was definitely intentionally cut?" This made me feel better and worse. Better, because that indicated our family magic hadn't been responsible for Donna's death, but then much worse, because this meant Donna had been murdered. At Jay's nod, I asked, "Could it have been done ahead of time and then the weight of Donna on the wire caused it to snap?"

Jay shook his head. "Our forensics team said it was sliced through—no evidence of the wire fraying at all."

"Marigold said there was a safety wire? What about that?"

We walked along the shore toward the festival grounds. We would have to weave our way up to Main Street for a block where there was no beach, but if we weren't taking a car, this was the fastest route.

"The safety wire wasn't much of a safety. It would have been too light to hold Donna's weight on its own, and it appeared to have been sliced through in the same manner."

We arrived at the vendor booths, which were all now cordoned off by yellow police tape. The entire road and beach had also been blocked off. Jay ducked under a strip of police tape and held it up so I could duck under it as well. Sherlock immediately headed for the water's edge. He wasn't a huge fan of water, so his quick change of direction told me that was where to find the evidence.

I felt eager to follow my cat, but Jay walked in the other direction, toward the Town Hall. There was one police officer keeping the area secure, but otherwise it was deserted and quite a mess. When people had left in a hurry last night, they left a plethora of fast food containers in their wake.

At the Town Hall, Jay pointed to the ground. "We're checking prints from the drink container believed to have belonged to Nate Miller."

Jay didn't give me much time to respond or to ask how long it would be to lift his fingerprints from the cup. Instead, he led the way up the outer rickety metal steps of the fire escape of the Town Hall, leading to the tiny platform at the top.

"He was also the first one on scene after Donna's fall last night."

"On scene? You mean on the reef?"

Jay nodded. That must have been the figure I'd seen in the rowboat only seconds after she fell to her death.

"As far as we can tell so far, you were the last one to see him before her fall, and at that point, he was arguing with Donna, which gives him possible motive. However, the fact that he arrived so quickly on scene, and from a rowboat, suggests he wouldn't have had time to be up near the wire at either end in order to cut it."

Once up on the top platform, I was surprised at the amount of metal clips and nylon strips strewn on the ground. Not only that, but much of the wire from the high-wire act last night had been gathered back up onto this platform, not so much in a spool, but in a messy pile.

"This is where Donna attached herself to the wire to launch across to the reef," he explained.

"What's all this?" I bent to look at the metal clips and nylon bits, but knew better than to touch anything, especially because they had been marked with tented, numbered cards by the forensics team.

"From what I understand, these are just extra screw-pin anchor shackles and carbineers, precautions to make sure they had the harnesses attached well."

"Precautions?" I had to repeat the word, and it came out angrier than I expected. *Precautions* should have meant that no one would have died.

Jay bent down beside me, his voice filled with compassion. "The harness was still perfectly intact when we found her."

I nodded, needing to do something to help figure this out. "So the harness was fine, and this was the end I'd seen Nate Miller at. Could he have gotten out to the reef before the big stunt without anyone seeing him?" This boyfriend of Donna's was the only serious suspect so far, so I couldn't help but latch onto him.

"It was dark, so he could have taken a boat from fifty feet on either side of the festival and he probably wouldn't have been spotted. But we saw him right out front, right after her fall."

"But without exact times, and without eyes on him the whole time, it's not impossible, right?"

"I suppose not."

I stood and looked at the pile of wire. "It's amazing that wire didn't kill anybody when it sprang back." When Jay looked at me, I added, "I mean, anybody else."

Jay pointed. "Because the cable was cut right near the end, it wasn't as wild by the time it got to shore. It could have been a lot worse, if someone had compromised it somewhere in the middle."

But of course, if it was cut, that would entail someone rising high above the ocean to cut it.

Jay led the way back down the stairs, to where Sherlock was now headed up. Jay gave him a concerned look. Even though I knew Sherlock wouldn't touch anything, I figured it couldn't hurt to put Jay's concerns to rest. "We're headed over to the reef next, right?" I pointed for Jay's benefit, as though my cat wouldn't understand my words. "To have a look at the scene of the crime."

Sherlock quickly turned from the stairs and led the way back toward the rocky shore, where two rowboats were still tethered to a small wharf. As we followed and Jay unhooked the rope securing one of the rowboats, I looked either way down the beach.

To my left, the marina was the closest place to dock a boat, and now, in daylight, it was partially visible and partially blocked by the tall rock face, dropping straight into the ocean. But there would have been no way for Nate Miller to have taken a boat out from the marina without Frank noticing. I knew for a fact that Frank had been around the marina last night, because he delivered a boat for the police to use only minutes after I called him.

The other direction, a wharf jutted out from the shore down near the town's brewery. I looked that direction, trying to imagine whether or not the wharf would have been out of sight by the light of only twinkle lights surrounding the festival. There was no boat there now, but perhaps there had been one moored last night.

"Here." Jay held out his hand to help me onto the boat. I'd gotten quite comfortable walking on and off of rocky boats since moving to Crystal Cove, but I didn't skip the chance to take Jay's hand. Murder investigations and family visits had held us back from anything romantic starting between us, but there was a strong sense that we both wanted it to, given the chance.

By the time I was aboard, Sherlock was sitting on his haunches on the front bench seat, centered, as though he planned to keep the whole thing for himself.

"Shove over," I told him, moving closer. He twitched his nose at me, which I imagined was cat language for an eye roll, but then at least he did as he was told and moved over a few inches.

He still took up the bulk of the bench, though, and when Jay started rowing, and the boat was obviously weighted to one side, I picked my cat up onto my lap and shimmied to the center, not caring if he had any kind of argument.

There weren't many places to moor near the reef. Last night, Aaron had been in such a hurry to get to Donna that he'd hopped out of the boat in his detective suit and his fellow officer had pulled the rowboat right up onto the rocks. I believe Nate Miller had done the same, although I couldn't recall for sure. Since then, they'd clearly navigated the reef more fully, and it was much easier to see during the day. Jay knew exactly where to go, and moments later, he had the boat attached to a post around the back of the reef, near the lighthouse, and he helped me out onto a large rock.

"Right up this way," he said, leading the way. It wasn't easy, finding footing over the rocks and I was glad I'd worn my hiking shoes with good grip.

As we neared the base of the lighthouse, I held my breath, suddenly feeling like we were about to come across Donna's dead body. We didn't, of course, but as soon as we rounded to the front of the lighthouse, there were dark markings on the rocks that I could only imagine would have been left from blood.

"This is where she died?" My voice came out shaky.

Jay moved beside me and rubbed my arm. "Yes." His voice was gentle.

I looked up, trying to divert myself to the investigation. I cleared my throat, mostly in an attempt to contain my emotions. "And that's where the wire was cut?" I tried not to process too carefully how many stories up it was to the platform at the top of the lighthouse.

Jay took my hand and led me toward the lighthouse entry. Still in his gentle voice, he said, "Come on."

I followed him through the stone door at the base of the lighthouse and up a spiral staircase that was only big enough for us to move single file. We stopped at a platform to catch our breath and then continued up another spiral staircase. And then another.

When we finally reached the open air at the top, six flights up, I was breathing so hard I had to gasp for a breath. But then I stood there stunned. We could see all of Crystal Cove from here. Besides the breathtaking beauty of the rocky shore and quaint town, I was struck by someone purposely performing a stunt this high up. I couldn't see what would motivate a person. It didn't seem safe.

"Why would Donna have taken the chance?" I whispered aloud, not able to hold back my thoughts.

Jay shook his head again. "I can't even guess." He motioned to some brown nylon material, which seemed to hook the wire rope to a concrete beam. "These are the nylon circles. Unbroken. The attachment to the screw-pin anchors are also intact."

I didn't know what any of that meant, only that it seemed like he was saying the attachments of the high wire had offered some measure of safety.

Again, there were tent cards from the forensics team everywhere. I squatted beside one with the number 17 on it, sitting beside what appeared to be a large battery. "What's this?"

Jay said, "It's a battery, likely for a drill." The battery had the name Rafuse on it, which I didn't recognize. "I expect they left it behind after they had rigged this whole high wire contraption."

"They?" I asked. "Who were they? Who set it up, and can we get their opinion on what happened?" My voice had taken on an angry tone. I wanted someone to blame for this.

Jay nodded. "We have a call into the town's head engineer. Aaron had a talk with Marigold Weathers this morning, and apparently he had helped the witches rig the whole thing, just to make sure it was safe."

Which, of course, it hadn't been.

But then I reminded myself that if someone hadn't cut Donna's wire, she would have been perfectly safe. She would still be alive.

Donna Davine had been murdered—beyond a shadow of a doubt. But I was still trying to come to terms with the fact.

Jay went on about the weight of the galvanized steel core wire rope and the unbroken nylon slings, and I just took deep breath after deep breath, trying to get my mind around this and think of who could be at fault, if not Nate Miller.

Why would she have even attempted this? I asked myself again. But this time I came up with an answer that I'd forgotten all about.

Marigold admitted she was looking for a new Queen Witch to take over for her in Crystal Cove.

Her death threats could be more connected than I initially thought, because could one of the local witches have been so disgruntled about Marigold choosing Donna over one of them, they'd have wanted to kill Donna?

"We need to make sure someone's watching Rachael," I said, panic in my voice. "She shouldn't be alone and asking questions if there's still a murderer out there somewhere."

Chapter Eight

WITH ONE PHONE CALL to Aaron, Jay put my mind at ease, at least some. "Aaron is heading over to Rachael's place himself. He thinks there's some validity to your theory and wants to go along with her to question the witches himself."

Any other time, I'd have laughed at the idea of Rachael and Aaron Thom, biggest magic skeptic of them all, conducting an investigation together among the local witches. But there was nothing to laugh about now. "And when they're done questioning the witches, what then? Will he still stay with her?" I was suddenly terrified for my young witch friend, who was somehow mixed into this investigation because of her artistic talents.

Jay nodded. "He will, or he'll bring in another officer to help." Jay kept a warm hand on my shoulder after he helped me back onto the boat.

As Jay took us back to shore, I felt dazed and had to say out loud the words I was trying to convince myself of. "So someone actually premeditated Donna's murder?" I didn't leave him time to answer. "Did you take fingerprints off of the apparatus? And the wire? And her broomstick?" I'd seen the broomstick now on the reef with another nearby tent card.

Jay nodded. "So far, we don't have any matches, but they'll only show up in our system if the person has a criminal record. I've put in a request to take prints from Marigold and the town engineer and anyone else who may have touched any of the apparatus, so we can rule those out and isolate prints from the guilty party, but at this point that doesn't help us if none of them are showing up in our system. Plus, the person could have been wearing gloves."

I looked up to the sky and sighed. It was gloomy today, looking like it could let out a downpour of rain, which mimicked my emotional state perfectly. As we arrived back at the wharf on shore, the feeling of helplessness overtook me. I had to do something to make sure Donna's killer was brought to justice. I had to.

"Have you asked Frank if anyone took a boat from the marina last night?"

Jay nodded. "He said the marina was completely quiet because everyone was at the festival."

Down the beach, Locality Brewery came back into view. I pointed. "Should we go and ask if there was a boat moored at their dock last night? It seems like the only way Nate Miller could have gotten across to the reef without being seen."

Jay gave me a look and opened his mouth. But then he nodded and said, "Sure."

I agreed with his sentiments. It did seem like a reach that Nate would have had time after arguing with Donna to get across to the reef and up to the top of the lighthouse and then back down and around the front of the reef so quickly after her fall. But I still had to check.

As we navigated across the large rocks toward the brewery, with Sherlock trailing behind us in order to sniff each and every rock, another thought occurred to me.

"Someone would have had to have been on the lighthouse side to help Donna dismount, right? Another witch, maybe?" I didn't like thinking one of the local witches could have actually premeditated Donna's death, but between the threats to Marigold, the clumsy attempt to frame Rachael, and now Donna's death, I had to face the possibility.

Jay shook his head. "There was a small ladder that was taken into evidence, which I assume had been placed there for her dismount. I can't imagine any of the local witches being strong enough to snap that wire with cable cutters, especially snapping it so cleanly."

"So we're looking for a man, then?" We continued walking. I tried to let myself feel some relief, but my chest felt tight with all my unanswered questions.

Jay nodded. "Or a strong woman."

This made me think of Marigold. Despite her sixty-something years, she was the strongest woman I knew. However, she'd been in plain view the whole evening. Even though she and Donna had had their differences in the past, they had been getting along well in the week leading up to the festival and Marigold had announced her as the new Queen Witch. I might have even called them besties, for how much time they'd spent together at the café lately.

We arrived at the beach side of the brewery, and Jay opened the heavy wooden door and held it open for me. I looked back at Sherlock, who was taking his time investigating rocks and still twenty feet back, and decided he'd be busy out here for the time it took us to get inside and ask a few questions. We walked up a set of stairs to the upper level, which looked out over the ocean.

"Hey, Connie," Jay called to a woman in her fifties behind a rustic wooden bar. During the day, the open seating area felt more like a café than a brewery, but I could imagine the ambiance changing at night. There were only two customers, a couple of men seated near the full-length windows. We moved past them toward Connie.

"Detective." Connie nodded with a smile. "Nice to see you. What can I get you and your lady friend?"

"Actually, this is my assistant." It was the first time he'd ever introduced me that way. Any other time, I might have felt disappointed by the distinction, but now, in the midst of the most personally important investigation I'd ever helped with, I felt honored to have an official title. "We're looking for an answer to a question or two." Jay had a casual way with this woman, and I guessed they had been crossing paths for years.

"You bet." Connie became instantly serious. "Just awful what happened at the solstice festival last night, wasn't it?"

Jay nodded. "That's what we have some questions about, actually." Connie put a hand to her chest in surprise, but Jay jumped in with his first question to circumvent where her thoughts might be going. "I was just wondering if you noticed a boat anchored at your wharf last night at any time?"

She glanced toward where Jay was pointing and then nodded. "Sure. Nate

Miller's boat was there for most of the evening."

"You're sure?" Jay asked

"Pretty sure. He stopped in around three that afternoon to ask if it was okay. Apparently, he wanted it to be ready for something or other later in the festival." She went on, but I could only look at Jay to see what he made of this.

"What time did he bring it by?" Jay asked. "And what time did he take it out that night?"

She sighed. "I spent most of the evening watching the festivities through the windows, but I'm afraid I couldn't say with any certainty what time Nate's boat was there, or when it wasn't. I can tell you for sure, though, that there weren't any other boats around our wharf that night."

Without any reaction, Jay thanked her and we left.

As soon as we were out the doors,
Jay held up a hand for me to stop, as
though he knew I was about to jump on
this information and lock up Nate Miller
before the clock struck noon.

"I'm putting in a call right now to
have someone track down Nate Miller
for questioning. The timing still doesn't
seem right, but I want to talk to the guy
in person and look for any red flags."

By this time, I'd calmed myself down
enough that I wouldn't spew a mouthful
of baseless claims at Jay. But I did
have one other thought that seemed
significant. "He was the first one out to
Donna. What if he tampered with the
evidence?" I wasn't even sure what kind
of evidence tampering I was suggesting.

Jay nodded, but didn't seem to have any
ideas about this either.

Back at the festival grounds, we
found Sherlock investigating the vendor
booths, but each one only seemed to

warrant a sniff or two before he moved along.

"I can't think of any way that Nate could have been at the top of the lighthouse at the time of Donna's death. Can you?" I asked. As far as I could figure, if we'd ruled out the local witches because of their lack of strength, he was not only our prime suspect, but our only one. Could he have been close to one of the other witches in town?

Jay shook his head. "There's something we're missing. But it'll turn up. You'll see."

Jay always had a lot more faith than I did when it came to solving seemingly unsolvable investigations. I didn't feel so sure.

"Do you want to come along with me to Happy Hardware to question CJ?"

"Sure, but why?" CJ was the sweet older man who owned Happy Hardware.

Jay shrugged and led the way back to the marina and his car. "I've heard rumors there was some tension between CJ and Donna. With Donna obviously murdered, I have to follow up on anyone with a possible motive."

I thought about this as I walked behind Jay. Did I really want to be a part of that interrogation?

But I wanted to find Donna's killer, no matter what. And I already said I would go.

Chapter Nine

On the way to Happy Hardware, Jay explained more about the tension between CJ and Donna.

"From what I understand, when she first rented her souvenir shop, she paid him to do some renovations. As you know, CJ's no spring chicken. From what I hear, the renovations took him a lot longer than anticipated. When he eventually completed them, Donna expected a discount for the time delay in opening her shop, but he actually charged her more, because it had taken so much time away from the hardware store."

"But that must have been years ago." I'd arrived in Crystal Cove almost a year ago, and Donna's shop seemed like a staple in town then.

Jay nodded. "But you know how arguments go in small towns." I was getting the idea of this, but he could probably see in my face that I didn't fully understand yet, so he went on to explain. "People pit their friends against one another, backtalk about each other's businesses. If the parties involved don't ever talk things out, these types of arguments can fester for decades."

"But is that enough reason for CJ to want to kill Donna? And why now, after all this time? Wouldn't he have done it years ago?" I shook my head at myself. "But honestly, could you even see CJ Donaldson as a coldblooded killer?"

Jay met my eyes as we crossed the street toward the hardware store. "Not even a little bit."

"But then why are we—"

"It's a lead we have to follow at the moment. And you know how this works, Tabby. One lead usually leads us to another. If we don't see any other options, we forge ahead with what we know."

"And Nate Miller? Maybe there's a way he could have gotten to the reef that we haven't thought about."

He nodded. "Aaron's having Officer Grant take the lead on that while he follows up with Rachael and the witches. We're finding other areas to dig in the meantime."

I wondered if Jay had purposely asked someone else to take over on investigating Nate Miller because I wasn't seeing reason. He put a hand on my arm as we arrived at the hardware store but didn't go in just yet. "We can talk to him later, too, if you still have questions." It sounded as though he was pacifying me.

And maybe Jay was right. Maybe Nate couldn't have been the guilty person. But who did that leave? Only everybody in town who we *didn't* see at the festival last night. Or someone who could have arrived at the reef hours before anyone was watching.

And, unfortunately, I had not seen CJ at the festival.

I sighed and followed Jay through the door. Sherlock followed me in and right up to the till, where CJ stood sorting some invoices. There were a couple of men at the rear of the store, but otherwise it was empty.

The sea glass around my neck stayed cool as Jay said, "Hello, CJ. I have a few questions and I wonder if you'd have a minute to answer them?"

CJ looked between me and Jay and down to Sherlock. Even though I'd been in his store many times, I'd never brought my cat inside. I opened my mouth to try to come up with some sort of an explanation of why I was doing it now, but CJ turned back to Jay before I could come up with anything.

"Sure thing," he said slowly. "Is this official police business, then?"

Jay nodded solemnly. "It is. Did you hear about what happened at the solstice festival last night?"

CJ bowed his head and shook it. "I still can't believe it." This didn't seem like the countenance of a man who had just gotten what he wanted by killing someone. But I understood police investigations well enough to know that a person's countenance wasn't enough to prove guilt or innocence.

"Can you tell me about your relationship with Donna Davine?" Jay asked.

CJ's eyes widened as he looked between me and Jay. CJ was a smart, intuitive man. It wasn't lost on him what this line of questioning might mean. "I—we didn't have a relationship. We barely spoke."

"Isn't it true you held a grudge against Donna Davine?" Jay waited through a long, uncomfortable silence.

"Yes, but I would have never have wanted her to get hurt."

Jay nodded and made a note on his notepad. "Can you tell me when you last saw her or spoke with her?"

CJ nodded, nothing but helpful. "She was in the store. About a month ago."

"And were you the one helping her?" At CJ's nod, Jay asked, "What day was this?"

CJ didn't have this information on the tip of his tongue, which might have been a good sign. He skimmed through his computer, and moments later said, "Just give me a minute. I'll be able to find it. She had been looking for some unusual items, so they shouldn't be hard to spot within our invoices."

"Unusual items?" Jay and I both asked at once.

"Here it is." CJ pointed to the screen. "She was in on December the second, looking for a specific type of cable wire that we didn't normally carry in the store here. I had some on hand from the last time Marigold had me order it, but it wasn't long enough for what Donna requested. I ended up having to order it from my supplier and paying an arm and a leg for them to ship it quickly."

His explanation raised several red flags, but I jumped on this one: "Did you argue with Donna about this rush order?"

The way CJ shifted his weight back and forth told me everything I needed to know. I wanted to sigh or shake my head, or leave this store before this questioning became any worse for CJ, but like Jay had said, we had to start with any possible lead, and right now that was our local hardware store manager. I had to believe that if we kept digging deeper, we would eventually be able to prove CJ's innocence.

"We did," he said slowly. "But mainly because I didn't think she'd be willing to cover the cost of the rush shipping. She had brought the town engineer in with her to place the order, to ensure everything she ordered was correct, and so our arguing hadn't gotten heated. She ended up prepaying for the shipping, stating the cost was far less important than her safety, and she'd be willing to pay a pretty penny to make sure all of their events at an upcoming festival were perfectly safe." CJ let out a sad sigh. "That's exactly how she'd phrased it—A pretty penny."

I could practically hear Donna's voice. She always spoke more like a middle-aged woman than like someone of her own young age.

"Had you had any problem getting her to pay, once the supplies arrived?"

CJ shook his head. "I wasn't in, but my clerk, Andy, charged her the price

I'd quoted and apparently she'd paid it without question."

"So you hadn't seen Donna since the second of December?" When CJ nodded his agreement, Jay added, "And this engineer was Henry McGill?"

"Yes, he works for the town as their head engineer."

Jay didn't bother making a note, which meant he must have already been aware of the man. "Did you see her at all on Saturday, at the festival?"

CJ shook his head. "I didn't attend, and I have to admit, I'm glad I didn't." He let out another sad sigh. "Just awful what happened." His face pinched. "Wait, surely you don't think I sold Donna faulty equipment? I ordered exactly what she asked for, and I didn't even open the package from my supplier! If you have concerns, you should follow up with them or with Henry McGill." He rifled through a pile of papers until he came across a glossy catalogue. "Here. This is where I ordered from." He slid it across the counter toward Jay, but Jay didn't reach for it.

"That won't be necessary, CJ. We are not suggesting faulty equipment."

CJ let out his breath, but then his gaze snapped back up to Jay. "Was it faulty rigging then? I wasn't there, so I assumed she'd just fallen off, but then why so many questions about her equipment?"

"We're just trying to get a full picture of the evening," Jay explained in vague terms, as he usually did when there was a murder at play. "On that note, you said you didn't attend the witches' solstice festival. Can you tell me where you were Saturday evening?"

"I was at home." CJ's eyes moved back and forth over Jay's as if trying to read into his questions.

"At home alone?" Jay confirmed, while making a note. I watched CJ carefully. He appeared worried more than guilty.

"Yes. I live on my own," he confirmed.

"You didn't go anywhere near the festival? Or perhaps take a boat out onto the water Saturday night?" Jay asked.

CJ's brow furrowed. "I left the shop at six and went straight home. I don't particularly like crowds, and I never go boating."

"Why is that?" Jay's question brought on some fast blinking from CJ. My hope of clearing him from suspicion was dwindling by the second.

It seemed CJ needed a moment to collect himself. When he finally spoke, he said, "I don't care for the water."

"Is this a fear?" Jay lowered his voice, still keeping to his business tone, but now with a hint of compassion.

CJ nodded and looked at his feet. "My younger brother, he fell out of a boat and drowned when he was seven. I haven't gone near the water since."

Either CJ was innocent, because there was no way to get to the reef except by water, or he was the best actor on the planet.

I guess Jay agreed, because he changed his line of questioning. "Do you know anyone else in town who had a contentious relationship with Donna Davine?"

CJ looked up at the ceiling as he searched for an answer. "No one I can think of, besides her on-again-off-again friendship with Marigold Weathers. But Marigold was the one who wrote out the list of supplies Donna needed, so I'm quite sure they were on good terms in the last month."

I could confirm that.

CJ's forehead creased again, and I could sense he was starting to clue into the fact that we were concerned over who didn't like Donna Davine and what that might mean.

"Thank you, CJ. If we have more questions, we'll be in touch."

As Jay started to say goodbye, my sea glass warmed around my neck. There was more to learn here. With a sudden burst of inspiration, I asked, "Did Donna only purchase the cable from you, or were there other items?"

CJ looked at me for a long moment as he registered he wasn't done being interrogated. Then he glanced at his computer screen. "There were lots of items." He turned the screen so it faced us. Her invoice listed a dozen or so bolts and hooks and anchors with long names, which made them seem very specific. "The cable was the only one I had to order in for her specially."

Jay scanned the list, seemingly recognizing a lot more in it than I did. He snapped a photo with his phone. "And what about the installation equipment? Did she purchase a drill or rent any other equipment from you?"

CJ shook his head. "No, but this sort of apparatus wouldn't require a drill. I recall her mentioning the nylon slings would serve so they could avoid any complicated drill work."

Jay rubbed his face, and then he navigated to something else on his phone. He turned the screen to show CJ. "We found this up near where the apparatus was installed. It's a drill battery, isn't it?"

CJ started to nod, but then he grabbed Jay's phone, pulled it closer, and used his thumb and forefinger to zoom in on the photo of the battery. A second later, he looked up and said, "I don't carry Rafuse products in store here. It's a high-end brand that makes mostly unique portable tools for odd jobs."

"Unique?" Jay and I asked at once.

CJ typed into his computer, and a moment later he had the Rafuse equipment website loaded. He pointed through a list of pictured items, including something called a track saw and a rotary hammer. When he got to the third item, Jay called, "Stop," before he had time to scroll past it.

Jay and I both bent closer to look at the twenty volt Rafuse pistol-grip cordless cable cutter. "Cable cutter?" I asked, in barely a whisper.

Jay cleared his throat and placed his phone back down in front of CJ. "Would the cable cutter use this type of battery?"

CJ zoomed even closer on Jay's phone, found a model number and then typed it into the Rafuse website. When he looked up at us, his tone was serious, although I suspected he didn't yet know how important this was. "That's exactly the type of battery it would take."

"And where would a person purchase such a tool?" Jay asked.

CJ's eyebrows rose as he thought about it. "Maybe Portland. Maybe online. But these cost upward of two thousand dollars, and to be honest, they wouldn't be useful for a whole lot of jobs. I can't imagine Donna or Marigold owning one."

This begged a couple of new questions: Had this Henry McGill actually constructed the high wire? I had initially thought the witches had installed it, but the more I learned about the intricacies of setting it up, I doubted they'd done it themselves.

But also, perhaps we couldn't rule out the other witches in town after all. When we'd thought about using manual cable cutters, it made sense that it would have to have been a strong man. With this pistol-grip cable cutter, anyone could have cut the wire while Donna was on it, perhaps even single-handedly.

The witches were suspects again. That seemed to put us back at square one.

Chapter Ten

By the time we finished up with CJ and arrived back at the marina, I was surprised to see it was almost time for my shift at The Heirloom Café. I'd asked Olivia for the weekend off, because my sister would be in town, but she'd been really short with me and told me she'd give me Saturday night off for the solstice festival, but that was the best she could do.

Olivia's moodiness could be frustrating, but Pepper assured me she only wanted to chill out. She didn't want me treating her like a tourist. She wanted to be a fly on the wall in my life.

Still, I groaned and said, "I wish I didn't have to work" to Jay. It was truer now than it had been when I thought I'd only be entertaining my sister. "How can I serve coffee when Donna was just murdered?" I'd meant the question as rhetorical, but Jay answered it anyway.

"Come on, Tabby. In the past, you've been able to listen in on some very useful information at that café."

I sighed, because he was right. People tended to get chatty at the café and say more than they probably would otherwise. Plus, many of the people people who frequented the café knew Donna Davine a lot better than I did.

Jay nudged my shoulder. "Go to your shift and text me when you're done. We'll compare notes and see if we can find someone other than CJ or Nate Miller to pursue."

I held my tongue from mentioning the local witches again. Many of them had become my friends in the last nine months, and even if some of them could be catty, I hoped none of them were capable of murder. It wasn't as though I didn't trust Rachael and Aaron to clear all of them from suspicion, but I also wanted to get my own vibe if any of them were at the café.

I said goodbye, and watched Jay drive off before heading back to the *Lady of Fortune*.

As I walked up the side wharf that led to my boat, I didn't see Pepper on the front deck until she said, "An early morning date? It must be serious."

My face warmed. I opened my mouth to deny it, but then closed it again and just shrugged. If she thought it was a date, she wouldn't pry for details about the investigation. Besides, getting serious with Jay Jameson was not a new thought, at least in my mind.

"Early morning was the only time I had available today. Remember, I have to work this afternoon?" I said, hoping my change of subject was seamless.

"Oh, right." Pepper pouted out her lips. Even though she'd told me on the phone that I should keep my shifts, I could tell now that she'd been keeping her real feelings on the subject a secret. She wished I didn't have to work.

"You can come and hang out at the café. For as long as you want."

She raised an eyebrow, like that didn't sound like much fun. However, I would have to find a time to ask her about the blue crystal and whether she had taken it from its box, and if I was being honest, I'd rather talk about that subject away from the boat.

Besides, I really was in a hurry to get to work.

❧

Forty minutes later, I rushed through the café doors, hair still damp from the shower. I was about to apologize for being five minutes late, but stopped myself when I saw Oliva huddled toward an attractive man in a suit at the front counter, her eyebrows pulled tightly together. He had a perfectly trimmed goatee and thick dark hair.

In my rush, I came upon them too quickly and heard Olivia say the words, "You have to know it's a sign," before she looked up and caught sight of me. The man followed her gaze and I was temporarily stunned by his piercing blue eyes.

"I—um—I'm sorry I'm late." I moved behind the counter barrier. "But I'm here now, so feel free to go...talk." I waved a hand like I was a game show hostess. Acting casual when I didn't feel casual was not my strong suit.

But Olivia having a hushed conversation with an attractive man? That was something so unusual that I simply couldn't contain myself, especially in my rushed and frazzled state.

They stared at me for a long moment, but then got back to their conversation exactly where they were. My emotions warred within me, wanting to give them privacy, but also wanting to lurk a little closer under the guise of prepping sandwiches for the afternoon.

I took my time stashing my purse and trying to decide, but by the time I turned back toward them, the man was heading for the door.

Olivia watched him go, and her countenance looked troubled and yet...swoony.

When the door closed behind him and she kept staring, I came up behind her. "Who's the good-looking guy?" I asked. Eventually, she pulled her gaze from the door and turned her blue eyes on me.

That was when it occurred to me. "Wait, is he your brother?"

A million thoughts raced through my head at once. Olivia had always been private about her family and her background. She was an attractive woman, but I wondered what it would be like having a sibling as attractive as that guy. Did she grow up with people befriending her, just to get to her brother?

But my rabbit-trailing brain stopped dead when Olivia shook her head and said, "That's Reg Carlson, my ex-boyfriend." Olivia spoke about her love interests even less than she spoke about her family.

"Wow." My mind reeled on what might have happened between them. Had he left her for another woman? Was he a player or did he struggle with commitment? Did he have a horrible personality, or a grating voice? When I couldn't land on my own explanation that felt right, I said the only word that came to mind again. "Wow."

She nodded, looking back at the door. "We dated for two years, but I wasn't willing to sell the café and move to Eugene, where he lives, and he wasn't willing to move here." It was the most Olivia had ever told me about her personal life. I stayed stock still and silent, hoping she'd go on. Eventually, she added, "Or he wasn't willing at the time."

I grinned as understanding bloomed. "He's come back for you? And wants to make a life with you here?" I'd always been a hopeless romantic, a sucker for a happy ending, at least when it came to other people's love lives.

But she shook her head. "It's not as simple as that."

This made me remember their tense posture when I'd interrupted them. And what had Olivia said? Something about a sign?

I figured she was about to clam up on me again, so I might as well ask. "But you think the universe is giving you a sign that you shouldn't be with him?"

She stared at me with wide, concerned eyes for a long time. So long that I worried I'd said something horribly wrong, and I expected her next words would be to tell me I was fired, or at the very least, to mind my own business. But then she told me the truth.

"He called me last night when he got into town." Her words were barely more than a whisper. "I had just locked up the café, and had headed home to change and then go to the festival. He met me downtown, but before we'd even arrived at the festival, people were leaving, some of them inconsolable, and then I heard what happened to Donna."

Olivia didn't always get along with the local witch coven, but I knew in that second that her heart hurt from losing anyone who frequented the café.

But surely she didn't think that this ex-boyfriend's visit, coming on the heels of Donna's death was any kind of a sign.

I wanted to tell her it was no accident—that this wasn't any kind of a sign from the universe, because it had been cold-blooded murder.

But it wasn't my place to share case details.

Instead, I said, "But, Olivia, one has nothing to do with the other. If the love of your life is back and he wants to leave everything behind to be with you—"

"Donna never trusted Reg," she said, cutting me off. "Back when we were dating, she told me several times I should find someone else, that I should stay away from him. Last night, when several locals rushed past us and I deduced what had happened to her... and then Reg being here so unexpectedly... the coincidence shook me, and I told him I'd have to talk to him today. But by the time he came by,

I knew it had been a sign to stay away from him."

Sign? Coincidence? I didn't think either of those things were true and it seemed unlike business-minded Olivia to talk this way.

Jay was right. I'd barely even arrived at the café, and I already had another angle to investigate on this case.

I'd found someone else who'd had contention with Donna, which automatically made him another suspect.

Chapter Eleven

Unfortunately, Olivia got quiet when I tried to ask her anything else about her ex-boyfriend, Reg, and soon after that, she left the café, saying she had to get to the farmer's market before it closed.

The farmer's market did close at two, but it still felt more like an excuse than a true obligation. I texted Jay right away, asking him to drop by when he had a minute, and then I was bombarded with the afternoon rush, so much so that I didn't even have time to Google Reg Carlson.

I didn't hear anything from Jay for several hours, and it was after dark when he and Pepper both walked into the café at the same time. Jay held the door open for her, smiles erupting on both of their faces as recognition hit and they became instantly chatty.

Great. Now that I really needed to speak to Jay privately, not only was I too busy to do so, but I wouldn't be able to keep the conversation away from my sister. It was already Sunday evening, and as much as I loved my sister, I wondered if she planned on leaving in the morning.

To my further dismay, they took a table together. I finished making up orders for the people at the counter, and in between those, I concocted a couple of caffeine-free hot drinks for them, since they still hadn't made their way to the counter to order anything. The more time went on, the more it concerned me that they—two nearly complete strangers—were so comfortable chatting without me. Did Jay think I'd told my sister all about the case, and so he felt free to share details? Or were they discussing me?

I didn't know which option bothered me more.

When I had a couple of decaf buttered rum lattes prepared, thankfully I had enough time to deliver them. By this time, Jay and Pepper were leaned across the table toward one another, almost conspiratorially.

Worse, when I appeared between them, they practically sprung apart.

"What's got you two so immersed?" I asked, forcing a chuckle to try and make my tone seem casual. It wasn't as though I thought Pepper might be interested in Jay, or vice versa. I just hoped she wasn't joking with him about all of my inadequacies.

Actually, when I really thought about it, this was how I could see their conversations about me going:

Jay: Tabby's been really talented at helping me with murder investigations.

Pepper: Tabby? Tabitha Chase, my sister? How is it that she's helping? Because she normally can't do much without our dad telling her exactly what to do, not to mention she can't stand the sight of blood or anything scary at all.

Jay: Hmm, that doesn't sound like the Tabby I know, but maybe I should pay a little closer attention.

Pepper: You definitely should. You'll see.

I tried to shake off my inner imaginings. They both thanked me for their drinks and stared up at me as I tried to bring myself back from this little self-made drama.

"You had something to tell me about the investigation?" Jay asked, almost knocking me out of my daze, but I still felt a strong urge to play out other possible scenarios in my head.

"Uh, yeah…" I looked between Jay and Pepper, and only a second later, Pepper popped out of her chair. "Are those the restrooms?" She pointed and didn't wait for my answer. "I've been drinking grapefruit juice all day." She skittered off toward the door marked for women.

I'd bought a whole carton of grapefruit juice because it was Pepper's favorite and she'd told me more than once that she couldn't find it anywhere on campus, so this wasn't completely implausible.

But as soon as she'd cleared out of the way, I slid into her seat and focused on Jay. "Did you tell her anything about the investigation?"

He ran a hand through his hair. "Not really, no. But she was there last night, and I did mention we had been around town asking questions this morning. She may have put the two together."

I thought again of the conversation I'd envisioned between them. But whatever my sister had told Jay, it didn't seem to have shaken his faith in me. I figured we may only have a few minutes, so I told him quickly, "When I came into the café, Olivia was arguing with an ex-boyfriend of hers."

Jay lifted an eyebrow. He knew I wasn't one to simply gossip, but he couldn't see the relevance.

"This ex-boyfriend had a contentious past with Donna Davine, and he happened to have shown up in town last night, out of the blue." I quickly gave him the rundown of the whole conversation. "His name is Reg Carlson, from Eugene, Oregon. Can you look into him?"

Jay agreed and made a note in his phone, since he didn't have his briefcase or notepad with him.

"Did you discover anything new today?" I fought the urge to pester him about why it had taken him all day to get back to me.

"Thom took Rachael to meet with a few of the local witches. Several of them mentioned they still didn't trust Marigold, but none of them had proof of any actual wrongdoing. So far, they've also all had alibis for the time of the murder."

I nodded, trying not to let my relief show. I'd much rather tag someone like Reg Carlson with the title of Prime Suspect.

"Once I added details about the cable cutter battery into evidence, the forensics guys came back to me, being able to connect some metal shavings they'd sampled from the upper lighthouse platform." So all signs were leading to this being the murder weapon. At this news, I was surprised when he suddenly changed topics. "Then I had to go up into the woods on another case. My cell reception was spotty, so I'm sorry I didn't get back to you sooner," he said, reading my mind as usual.

My sea glass warmed, and I wondered if it was telling me I was supposed to help with that investigation as well.

But only a second later, Pepper appeared over my shoulder, and I realized the sea glass warmth was only a warning to watch what I said.

"Stealing my chair?" Pepper asked. "I'll bet you drank my whole drink, too."

I hadn't, and I knew she was only teasing, but before I could say anything, Jay stood. "I'd better take mine to go. But thanks, Tabby." He held up his latte. "For the drink and for the information."

He left, and Pepper started to ask, "What information did you give him—" but before she fully had the question out, a customer wandered up to the counter, wanting a muffin from our baking display.

I smiled at how the universe worked something in my favor once in a while and rushed over to fill the person's order.

As more customers came at me, I felt a sudden sense of overwhelm, as though

I couldn't handle a few customers in a row, even though I'd handled many heavier rushes in the past.

My sea glass also remained warm against my collarbone, and I couldn't shake the feeling that something wasn't quite right here. I just couldn't put my finger on what.

I served another three or four customers—I couldn't even keep straight how many—and then it finally occurred to me.

The blue crystal.

Did Pepper have it with her now?

Chapter Twelve

PEPPER STAYED UNTIL CLOSING, and I spent the entire time trying to keep my head straight enough to serve customers and decide how to demand some answers from her without freaking her out in the process.

Without me having asked, she'd grabbed a broom to sweep up the café as I locked the door behind the last customers. I headed behind the counter to count up the cash register. Olivia would be here any minute. She always insisted on officially closing up herself, and in fact, I was surprised she was running so late today.

I was halfway through counting up the five-dollar bills when I lost count and had to start over. Then the same thing happened on the quarters, and the dimes. I was so scatterbrained—

My gaze landed on my sister's brown leather purse, slung over the back of a nearby chair, and as the thought hit me, it launched, unstoppable, out of my mouth. "You have it, don't you?" She stopped sweeping and stared at the floor. "You have the blue crystal from my bedroom closet."

She began to sweep again, but I didn't miss the blush that rose up her neck. My sister had always been a fan of shiny, sparkly things, so the fact that she helped herself to a jewel she'd found in the back of my closet wasn't the surprising part. What I couldn't get over was how well she was functioning, if she indeed had the jewel so close to her.

I looked from her jeans pockets, which appeared to be too snug to hold the crystal, and back to her purse.

Without waiting for her answer, I started to count in my head, to keep my mind straight, and headed straight for her purse. She was saying something—apologizing or mentioning how she was going to ask me about it—but I couldn't tune into any of her words. I had to keep focused on my counting.

As I opened her purse, I counted aloud. I had to. "Seventeen, eighteen, nineteen..." And there it was, no longer in its box, but now wrapped in a floral napkin, one of the ones I kept near my aunt's table.

Pepper was still rattling off apologies to me, but I held up a finger in her direction and moved straight to the back storage room. I pulled out a can of mixed beans from the bottom shelf and stuck the crystal and the napkin behind the can.

Olivia used the beans for chili, but she only made chili once every three months or so. The crystal would be safe for a little while.

When I walked back through the door into the café, Pepper had replaced the broom, but was frantically straightening chairs. I could think better now, but I wondered if she couldn't, because she didn't seem herself. I stopped her, grabbing her by the shoulders and turning her to face me. She had tears in her eyes.

"Pepps, it's okay. Now that it's in the back room, just take a few breaths and you should be able to concentrate again." I mimicked taking a big yoga breath and pushing it out slowly through my lips.

But she stared straight at me and her eyes flooded with more tears. "I can concentrate just fine," she said in a tone that I remembered well from our childhood. It was the tone she used when she was fighting over the TV remote from either me or our brother, Zach, or when she came home from school assuring us that she didn't want to be friends with the girls who hadn't asked her to sit with them at lunch.

This was Pepper's jealousy.

Before I could come up with the right words to calm her down, she let out plenty of words that seemed right on the tip of her tongue.

"Mom thought I needed some preparation for the strange things that go on in Crystal Cove. She said if I found any jewels around the boat, I should treat them carefully and ask you if I had any questions about what I experienced from them, but I didn't have any questions, because nothing happened!"

I blinked a couple of times, trying to catch up. "The blue crystal doesn't affect you?"

She looked as though my words might as well have slapped her.

"I was here for months before I understood any of it, Pepper. In fact, I still don't understand most of it, and believe me, if you're not feeling anything, it has nothing to do with you not being good enough." Whether or not that was true, I honestly didn't know, but what I did know was how much my sister needed some reassurance right now.

"And what about that." She pointed at my sea glass. "You never take it off. It gives you powers, doesn't it?"

I shook my head, but didn't have time to answer Pepper, because right then, Olivia's key sounded in the door.

Not only that, but as Olivia moved inside, she wasn't alone.

Reg Carlson was with her and my sea glass instantly burned against my collar bone.

Chapter Thirteen

I WAS TORN ABOUT what to do. I turned back to Pepper, as she wasn't going to be of much help in her emotional state, but thankfully she had wiped her tears and looked surprisingly presentable.

"Olivia's here to lock up," I told her. "Let's talk about this more back on the boat."

Pepper nodded, but then she turned toward the storage room door.

"It'll be fine," I murmured quietly. Olivia wouldn't be making chili before my shift tomorrow.

As we gathered up our purses, Olivia and Reg were both silent, apparently unwilling to say a single word in front of us. I might have respected their wishes if I hadn't been concerned about Reg being a suspected murderer.

"I didn't realize you had company tonight," I told Olivia. "I could have locked up on my own."

She waved a hand. "No need. Reg and I were out for a walk and it took us longer than I expected to get here from Locality Brewery."

I raised my eyebrows. "You went by Locality Brewery tonight?" I couldn't help repeating her words. Not only was it coincidental that Jay and I had been there earlier today, but the brewery also perfectly overlooked the festival grounds where Donna had been killed. It was as though Reg had brought her there as a way of gloating over what he'd done.

Or was I getting ahead of myself?

I had the sudden urge to stay close to Olivia's side, so I stuck out my hand toward Reg. "I'm Tabby. I've lived in town here for almost a year and have been getting to know Olivia pretty well." This was definitely stretching the truth, and yet I let the words stand. I wanted Reg to feel as though someone was keeping an eye on him, now that Donna wasn't around to do it.

"Reg. Carlson." He shook my hand, but then pulled his quickly back and looked to Olivia, like he was wondering why I was bothering him. The guy seemed less attractive and jumpier tonight than he had earlier.

"You're a beer drinker then?" I asked him. "What did you think of Locality's lager?"

In truth, I didn't know if they even brewed a lager, but Reg said, "Not one for beer, myself, but the view from their upper level is pretty spectacular."

A spectacularly morbid view, if you asked me.

"Plus, their food is really good," Olivia put in, sounding uncomfortable by this conversation. "Have you eaten there, Tabby?"

I started to shake my head, but Olivia didn't leave time for me to answer. "I'll have to take you there sometime." Now this was definitely strange. In the entire time I'd known her, Olivia had never taken me out anywhere, or even suggested such a thing. She headed for the door and held it open for us. "I'll see you tomorrow."

Our conversation, apparently, was over. She didn't ask if this was my sister, the one I'd been talking about all week, or introduce herself. Seconds later, I stood out on the sidewalk beside Pepper, stunned by her strangeness.

"She sure seemed in a hurry for us to leave." Pepper raised an eyebrow, still staring at the door from beside me. It had to mean something that even Pepper noticed Olivia's abruptness. She turned toward the marina and started walking, but I stayed rooted in place, pulling out my phone and navigating to Jay's contact.

I had typed half of my text message before Pepper realized she'd lost me and came back to see what was wrong. I finished up my message and hit send.

"What's up?" she asked.

I figured it couldn't hurt to be honest, since I'd likely be worrying about this all night. "I don't know that I trust that guy Olivia's with. Donna Davine never liked him, and I texted Jay to see if he knows anything about the guy." It was a half-truth, since I'd given Jay Reg's name earlier. I had texted that Olivia and Reg had gone to the brewery earlier, and that they were currently in the café and I was worried about leaving her alone with him.

"Donna Davine? The witch who fell last night?" At my nod, she asked, "Do you think you should call Olivia? Give her an out?" Pepper and I used to have a system back when we were barely out of high school. When one of us went on a date, the other always called an hour or so in. That way, if the date wasn't working out, we could feign some sort of emergency.

"Good idea." As I navigated to Olivia's number, Pepper pulled me down the sidewalk and out of sight. She was much better at playing inconspicuous when it came to people we knew.

Olivia picked up after two rings. "Tabby? What's up? Did you forget something?"

I took a big breath and tried to keep my voice steady. "Not exactly, but… You're not on speakerphone, are you?"

"No…" Her voice sounded wary.

"I just… I left with a bad feeling, and I wanted to make sure you felt safe. I wasn't sure I should leave you alone."

She heaved out a sigh. "Not you, too. Look, Tabby, I'm fine. Reg just wants a little uninterrupted time to talk, which

I have to admit, I'm having trouble finding."

I gnawed at my lip, torn. But then Olivia made the decision for me.

"I appreciate your concern, but this isn't your business, Tabby. I'll talk to you tomorrow."

And with that, she hung up.

Chapter Fourteen

I HAD BARELY REGISTERED that Olivia had hung up on me when Pepper asked, "What did she say?" at the same time a new text came through from Jay.

I held up a finger to Pepper and read Jay's text.

I'm not far from the café. I'll go run into them by "chance" and investigate a little. He co-owns a shipping company out of Eugene. The guy doesn't have a record, but that doesn't always mean anything.

I let out a breath, glad Jay was being cautious. Then I typed back: **I'm just**

outside. Should I stick around and help?

My disappointment was palpable when his response came.

Probably better if you clear out. Olivia Bertram can be jumpy and closed off at the best of times.

I responded with a thumbs-up emoji, as that was the only way I could appear positive and upbeat when I felt disappointed. I started walking toward the marina, not wanting to ruin his "chance" meetup.

I was surprised at his assessment of Olivia. It was dead on, but he always seemed so pleasant with her. It had never occurred to me that he had read deeper into her and her personality.

"So now you're just going to leave her here?" Pepper asked, too loud, as she jogged to catch up to me.

I shushed her, and kept my voice low as I said, "Jay is on it, and he'd prefer

if we cleared out before he got here."
I had to admit, it made me feel slightly better to use the pronoun "we." At least Pepper and I were both unwanted here, or so I told myself, even though I hadn't mentioned her in any of my texts.

When the marina came into view, I decided it would get both of our minds off of Reg Carlson to get back onto the topic of Pepper and the blue crystal. As we boarded the *Lady of Fortune,* I had complete clarity over the questions I should ask, too, but then Pepper surprised me by asking the first one.

"So was Mom just teasing me, or what? There's no real magic around this place, is there?"

As I set my purse down, I touched my sea glass. I didn't want to hurt Pepper's feelings, and I wondered if it was truly worth getting into the whole idea of trying to convince her that magic was real at almost eleven o'clock at night, especially when she hadn't felt any.

But this was my sister. We had always been honest with one another, and as my sea glass warmed, it felt like an encouragement.

"To be honest, Pepps, I had a really hard time figuring out what was real and what was make believe when I first moved here. There are still things that stretch my beliefs and are beyond my understanding."

"Including that blue crystal?" She raised an eyebrow in challenge.

"Yes, in fact, that piece is the most powerful one I've come into contact with since moving here."

She crossed her arms. "And yet it hasn't done a thing for me. I've been keeping it right at my side since early last night, and I haven't seen a single unusual occurrence. Well, except for that witch falling to her death, but—" Her eyes met mine in horror as she spoke the words. "Wait, I was rubbing the jewel in my coat pocket, since I was so nervous watching the witch on that tiny wire. You don't think…"

"No, Pepper. You didn't do that to Donna." I knew I should keep quiet about Jay finding evidence of the cut wire. "Crystal Cove's magic didn't do that. I don't know everything about the strange town happenings yet, not by a long shot, but I can tell you that everything I've seen from Crystal Cove's true magic and the magic that Aunt Lizzie used—it was always aimed at doing good."

Pepper sunk down onto the purple loveseat. "So Aunt Lizzie wasn't crazy?"

I knew that was how my brother and sister had always viewed our aunt, a sentiment passed down from our father. I suddenly felt bad for our mom, who had listened to that about her sister for all those years, all while hearing the truth from Aunt Lizzie's own mouth.

As my sea glass warmed more around my neck, I had an idea. "You know, when I first moved to town, and first started to accept that magic could be a real thing, I couldn't think properly around the blue crystal. I still can't. It's too strong for me." I unlatched the chain at the back of my neck and held it out. "I started with this."

Maybe it was because it was late at night and I was tired, or maybe it was because I'd seen Pepper's anguish over her understanding of magic and what was true, but I no longer feared her ability with it. Explaining it to her had reminded me that Crystal Cove's magic really wasn't a power game or an evil force. It wasn't about backbiting witches who sometimes tried to pretend their magic was more powerful than it was. It was about being a force for good in this little town. The truth was, me alone, with my limited understanding—I wasn't enough.

Pepper hesitated, but then she reached for the necklace. She held it in her hand, but didn't attempt to put it on. After a long beat, she looked up at me. "I don't feel anything."

"No, you wouldn't." She immediately looked wounded at my words, so I went on. "I mean, it's not something I *feel* all the time. For me, the sea glass just enhances my intuition when I need it. It's been gently teaching me about magic, as if the magic knows how much I can handle."

Pepper let out a chuckle under her breath at this. "Well, if that's the case then it'll take a good long while to show me anything, won't it?" She got serious. "But it helps you, doesn't it? It helps you know things?"

I rubbed my chin. Her words didn't quite sound right. "Not know things, exactly."

She waved a hand like the distinction didn't matter. "I mean it helps you so that you can help Detective Jay with his investigations."

Most people in town called him Detective Jameson. Those who knew him really well called him Jay. I'd never heard

Detective Jay, but I liked it. "Is that what you two were talking about at the café?"

"He told me a lot of things," she said, full of innuendo. I couldn't tell if he'd genuinely told her things—like how he felt about me—or if she was only teasing. But before I could press her about it, my phone dinged. At eleven o'clock at night, it had to be Jay. I dashed for my purse, and then my phone, quickly scrolling through his words.

I waited twenty minutes until they left. Olivia seemed agitated, and so I stuck around and made sure she got into her own vehicle and went home alone. Reg claimed to have arrived in town after the incident Saturday night, but I'm not sure I believe him. For the moment, I have an officer watching his room at the Bayside Bed & Breakfast to ensure he doesn't bother Olivia again tonight. I think you could be right on this one.

As much as I appreciated the affirmation, I still felt worried about Olivia being so close to a murder suspect, and unwilling to hear any advice about being cautious.

Pepper moved behind me and read his text over my shoulder. I didn't stop her, as the more she learned about the truth of my life here, the better it felt to have someone to talk to.

"The guy was shifty, but I'm not sure he killed your witch friend," she eventually said.

Had Jay told her we were investigating a murder? Or was she just spit-balling? "No?" I raised my eyebrows at her and noticed she was rubbing the sea glass. She still hadn't put it on, and instead handed it back to me.

"Here. Feel."

I took the sea glass, and it was cool to the touch. I nodded. "I still feel better knowing that someone's watching him."

Pepper nodded. "Me too. Why did he come back to town to try and rekindle his romance with your boss last night? Why on the same night that a witch he disliked was killed?"

She was right. That seemed far too coincidental. "We should get some sleep. We'll think better after a good night's rest."

She agreed, and then told me, "And tomorrow you can make me my own sea glass necklace, because I think I'm getting to know exactly what you mean about it."

Chapter Fifteen

THE NEXT MORNING, I turned my phone on to see an early-morning text from Jay.

All's been quiet at the bed & breakfast. What's your schedule like today? Do you have time to take a drive with me?

I wrote back: **I work at 2. Enough time?**

A second later his reply came: **It'll be enough. Can your sister join us?**

I had to admit, I was surprised at this. It definitely didn't seem like a date, then. But could it have to do with the investigation, since I didn't think he'd be ready to fully involve Pepper?

I'd have to wake her, I typed back.

I was even more surprised by his reply. **Do that. We'll pick you both up in half an hour. Wear hiking clothes.**

We? Could he be planning some sort of a double date hike?

By the time Jay drove into the marina parking lot, Pepper and I were both waiting. Pepper still looked half asleep, with wet hair from the shower and bleary eyes, but when I'd shown her Jay's slew of texts, she hadn't argued or gotten upset with me for waking her. Sherlock sat on his haunches at Pepper's feet. It hadn't even been a question of whether or not he would join us, but I wondered how his short legs would fare if the hike was steep or rugged.

While we'd eaten a quick breakfast, I explained the one thing I needed her to know before going out with Jay:

That our family brand of magic couldn't be discussed with anyone outside the family.

She had nodded, but I honestly had no idea how much was going into her brain when she was barely awake. I wondered if the reason she'd been having so much trouble with school was because some of her hardest classes started at seven a.m. My sister had always been the night owl of the family.

As Jay drove closer, I saw Aaron Thom in the passenger seat. He'd barely stopped the car, when I opened one of the back doors and asked, "Who's watching Rachael?"

Jay looked over the seat at me. "It's okay, Tabby."

I nearly began ranting at him about how nothing was okay about leaving Rachael on her own after she'd been asking questions about Marigold's death threats, but Aaron spoke before I could say anything else.

"She has several house cleaning jobs today."

Again, I opened my mouth to tell him she wasn't safe, but once again, he cut me off.

"Officer Grant is driving her and watching over her for the day. She'll be safe, Tabby." While Jay was usually the more compassionate of the two police detectives, Aaron's voice right now was softer than usual. He clearly knew how worried I was about my friend.

"Hop in," Jay said, when he could tell I was calming down. "Help yourselves to a breakfast burrito."

Tortilla Street Grill covered the wrappers on the console. The restaurant was located at the end of Main Street and I hadn't eaten there yet, but I'd heard wonderful things about their food. I didn't hesitate to help myself to a roll wrapped in parchment paper.

Pepper wasn't as fast to grab one. We'd already had some granola for breakfast, but even with that, she'd barely eaten any. I chalked it up to her not being fully awake. "Where are we going?" she asked, her tone just on the edge of irritable. "On a hike?"

"Not exactly." Jay rubbed his hands back and forth on the steering wheel, like he didn't have the right words. "How much has Tabby told you about the investigation around Donna Davine's death?"

"Almost nothing!" I shot back, both offended that he'd think I didn't know to keep my mouth shut, especially with Aaron here, and embarrassed that I had been considering telling Pepper everything, all because of our shared magic.

As Jay pulled off the main road onto a dirt road that led into the mountains, he shook his head at me. "No, Tabby, I'm not..." He shook his head again, still struggling for words. Aaron tapped into his phone, not paying any attention.

Did this morning "hike" have something to do with the investigation into Donna's death? If so, I wished Jay had mentioned this first, and I could have told him Pepper didn't know anything. She could have slept in, and if he really wanted to bring her into the loop—for some reason I was yet to understand—we could have done that after our hike. I highly doubted Aaron Thom was here on any kind of double date, as he'd barely paid any attention to Pepper and me since we'd gotten into the car.

Jay finally found some words. "I thought it was best for both of you to be here." I still had no idea what that meant. Did he sense some magical prowess in my sister that even she couldn't feel yet? Did he just think four heads were better than three? He glanced up to his rearview mirror, so he could talk with Pepper, who sat directly behind him. "I'm not sure what you already know, but we are considering the incident from Saturday night a homicide."

Pepper blinked a few times, trying to wake herself up. "Murder? For real?"

So she had just been spit-balling last night.

Jay nodded, still watching her every chance he could look away from the road. "We found some evidence of cable cutters in the upper level of the lighthouse, and the cable Donna Davine had been flying on had been cleanly cut."

Pepper gasped. My heart ratcheted up, but for a different reason. The direction Jay was driving, on a dirt road up into the mountains, looked familiar. Shortly after I'd arrived in town, and after I'd gotten to know Jay, I'd asked him if he would take me to where Aunt Lizzie's body had been found. I had been more emotionally distraught at the time, and hadn't been paying a great deal of attention to the outskirts of what was a brand new town to me, but this looked so familiar, I couldn't shake it.

Jay was explaining more of his investigation to Pepper, but I interrupted. I had to know. "This looks like where Aunt Lizzie died."

Jay hesitated, but then nodded solemnly, now looking ahead, rather than at either of us.

Why were we going up there again? Had Pepper asked about seeing the area, too, and Jay didn't think he should bring her alone?

I fingered the sea glass around my neck, knowing that wasn't it.

This trip to where my aunt had died...for some reason it was closely related to Donna Davine's murder.

Jay drove as far as he could, mostly trying to keep me calm with promises to show us more when we got there. When he came to a narrowing of the road into a path, he pulled over as much as the road allowed and turned off his engine.

"This is why I thought you both should come along."

I still didn't know what "This" was. I'd barely tasted the breakfast burrito Jay had brought, with all my questions, and now it tumbled uneasily in my stomach.

"So we're hiking?" Pepper confirmed, still stuck on that part.

"It's not far," Jay assured her, getting out.

I hoped that once we got moving in the fresh, crisp air, Pepper would wake up enough to clue in to what was happening. I didn't want to go through this emotional turmoil alone.

The last time Jay had brought me up here, it was for me to find some closure. I'd told myself I'd found exactly that again and again. But as I got out of the car now, I realized that what I'd found hadn't been closure. It had been a firm decision to never have to look at this place again.

I swallowed hard. Jay was watching me carefully, as though he knew he was asking a lot.

"Is this really necessary?" I finally got out.

"I wish it wasn't, Tabby." He looked at the ground, but before he dropped his gaze I caught a sadness in his eyes. He didn't want to be here anymore than I did.

So why were we?

Without looking at me again, Jay turned and led the way to the path. "Come on. It's not far. Let's go."

Aaron finally put his phone away and followed Jay. He was usually one to take the lead on investigations, so I found it curious that he hadn't been the one to drive up here, and now he was following Jay's lead without a word. Maybe he didn't know any more about this than Pepper and me.

The hike wasn't far, but it was so steep that it kept us breathing heavily enough that we didn't want to talk. I didn't want to talk, regardless, and Pepper probably wasn't awake enough to talk. Sherlock slowly brought up the rear, but I was too busy steeling myself to worry about picking him up.

I was surprised, actually, at the steep incline, and momentarily wondered if Jay was bringing me somewhere different. Perhaps this road just looked a lot like the one that led to where Lizzie died. But, no. Jay had already confirmed it was the same place.

As we hiked in silence, my mind turned over things I hadn't let it think about in months. Aunt Lizzie had been a force in Crystal Cove when she'd been alive—a force for good. She'd had goals—to see the town united, and to break the barriers that kept people at odds. Even in her death, she'd had an uplifted spirit. Her suicide note had talked not about her suffering and pain; instead it had been all about flying into the great beyond.

Flying?

I stopped in place, and because Pepper was behind me, with her gaze on her feet, she stumbled right into me. "Tabby? What's up?"

Jay and Aaron stopped and looked back at us, but only for a second. Jay saw something on my face, turned back around, and called, "We're almost there. Come on. We'll talk about it soon."

Chapter Sixteen

THE REASON THIS PATH didn't look familiar became apparent when we arrived at the edge of a cliff. Trees rose up high above us, and as I gazed down over the precipice, I recognized the jagged rocks below, where Jay had brought me to the last time we were up here.

I looked at him in question.

"This was where her flight started." Jay looked to Pepper. His voice was gentle. "I believe your Aunt Lizzie had been attempting a similar stunt to Donna's when she fell."

"Wait, Fell? What?" I spun to Jay, full on. "I thought she jumped? That was what the police report said."

Jay nodded, solemnly. "That is what the report said. Police investigations aren't perfect," he glanced at Aaron, "and I've recently come across some additional information that makes me doubt our initial assessment."

Jay never usually spoke in such clinical terms, at least not with me. I wondered if it was only Aaron's presence that brought it out now, or if there was still something he wasn't telling me.

"What? What additional information?" My voice was abrupt, cold. I couldn't help myself.

At least it seemed that Pepper was finally waking up. "Are you saying our aunt never committed suicide? That's a big mistake to make!"

"What about her suicide note?" My question came right on top of Pepper's words. A very small part of me felt badly that we were ganging up on Jay, but the rest of me was overwhelmed by the hopeful thoughts warring to take over inside me. Because of course it would be infinitely better if Aunt Lizzie hadn't killed herself. But what if Jay was jumping the gun here?

Jay nodded and pulled out his phone. Whatever he was pulling up, Aaron had clearly already seen it, as his attention was now on the surrounding area. He moved away, looking from the rocks at the edge of the cliff, up to the nearby tree branches. Meanwhile, Jay scrolled through a few different screens before landing on something he wanted to show me and Pepper. He turned his phone to us and I blinked twice before quickly looking away.

Our mother had the suicide note that Aunt Lizzie had written. I'd had one brief glimpse at it, enough to recognize my aunt's handwriting, but beyond that, I hadn't been able to focus on it. It hurt too much.

While the original was with our mom, clearly, Jay still had a copy of the note on file.

Pepper pulled Jay's phone in front of her when she realized I had no desire to look at it.

"Flight... ? Great beyond...? After this, we'll all know?"

I squeezed my eyes shut, not wanting to hear Aunt Lizzie's specific words. Jay could probably tell that I wasn't doing a good job of taking in any of this.
He grabbed my hand and led me away while Pepper continued to pour over the suicide note—or perhaps just... note?

"I know this is hard to grasp after all this time," Jay told me quietly. "It was difficult for me, too."

Pepper, on the other hand, was now asking her questions aloud—"What does this mean, exactly? And what about that phrasing?" She seemed as detached as she did when she discussed questions from her medical texts. Then again, she hadn't come to stay on her own with Aunt Lizzie on her houseboat, not even once. They hadn't been nearly as close as Aunt Lizzie and I were.

Aaron moved beside her. "You can see how the suicide note, along with her fall didn't leave many questions for us last winter." His words held a hint of defensiveness. "Knowing what we do now, perhaps there are other interpretations we should have considered."

Jay went on, taking my attention. "Yesterday afternoon, I was going over all the evidence and photos from our forensics team, and I noticed something that looked familiar. Do you remember how the cable was attached to the lighthouse's concrete beam?" He reached into his pocket for his phone, but then glanced to Pepper, remembering that she had it.

But I remembered. "The nylon slings, so they didn't have to drill anything, right?"

"Exactly. Anyway, I came up here yesterday afternoon to see if it was a real memory, or if my mind was playing tricks on me." He led me father from the cliff and to the nearest tree. He pointed up.

I followed his finger to the branches, and I didn't see anything significant. Sherlock sniffed around the base of the tree.

"See that brown streak?" He brought his face close to mine and pointed so I was on the same angle as him. I didn't, but then he brought my hand up, to used it to point within the branches.

All of a sudden, I saw a small streak of brown that stood out among the branches of the nearest, tallest Douglas fir.

My head snapped to Jay. "What are you saying? Someone killed Lizzie the same way they killed Donna?" Had a serial killer been roaming freely in Crystal Cove for nearly a year?

But Jay shook his head as Pepper and Aaron joined us to hear what we were discussing. "I don't think so."

I grimaced, not understanding.

"I think your aunt fell and someone came out here to get rid of the wire and cover up the accident."

"Why would someone do that? Why make it look like a suicide?" I reached for Jay's phone, ready to look at the suicide note, now with a fresh understanding.

Jay stared up the tree. "I was hoping the two of you could help me figure that out."

Chapter Seventeen

Jay hadn't brought his discoveries back to anyone at the station yet. Bringing Aaron up here was his first step in doing so. "If I'm wrong, it would be really upsetting for you and your family if all of a sudden the case was reopened, and for nothing. But I brought a ladder out early this morning and a closer look indicated it's the same type of nylon sling." He glanced to Aaron. "I know I'll need to report in with this today and then the forensics team will confirm it. I guess I just hoped to discuss it with the three of you first."

I nodded, gazing around at the surrounding trees, as though they might tell the full story. Jay's care was obvious, and he'd had all night to process this, but what did it really mean? "Do you think the same person who killed Donna also made my aunt's death look like a suicide?" I asked, trying to keep my voice from wavering.

He shook his head. "At this point, I don't have any reason to believe that. However, there are definite similarities. I believe it was a stunt—"

"For who?" I interrupted. "There was no one out here when Aunt Lizzie died, right?"

Jay ran a hand along the bark of a nearby tree. I had a moment of wondering if fingerprints could be lifted from tree bark, but I guessed it was too late for that, even if they could. "There would have had to have been someone along to help her up to the wire," he said. "And someone who removed the wire from the scene before your aunt's body was discovered. By the time the police arrived that day, all evidence indicated it had only been a matter of a few hours since her death, so I can't see how she would have been up here completely alone."

"Well, clearly if the local witches had come out to watch her perform some kind of theatrics, someone would have mentioned it."

He nodded. "You're right. A crowd wasn't here. But that doesn't mean no one was here."

I thought of how Sheena and the other witch had helped Donna to get hoisted onto her broom and the high wire.

"But why?" Pepper asked. She looked from the tree trunk indentations to the rocks below. "Why cover it up?"

"My guess is that someone felt responsible, or perhaps *was* responsible for the fall."

We spent an hour investigating and taking photos of every angle of the tree trunk, the ground surrounding it, and then the lower rocky area that had already been fully investigated.

"Where would the cable have attached on this end?" I asked, looking around at the sturdiest trees.

Jay nodded. "I looked as best as I could, but last summer's brush fire marred the trunks and branches of many of the trees down here."

"But she fell last February," Pepper said.

"Yes, but back then we had no idea we were looking for any evidence within the trees. At the time, it seemed like a clear-cut suicide."

My emotions warred within me. Of course I was thankful to learn that Aunt Lizzie probably had not killed herself, but if that was the case, and if someone local had covered up her fall, or allowed it to look like a suicide, had they been hiding the evidence and keeping this to themselves for almost a year?

Unfortunately, when the idea of that hit me, only one name came to mind.

"I think we should go and have a thorough talk with Marigold about this."

Aaron and Jay looked to each other and nodded their agreement.

Chapter Eighteen

Sherlock and I followed at a distance back toward the car. My emotions warred within me, but more than anything, I wanted to give Sherlock a chance to voice his thoughts, and the moment we were out of earshot of the others, he didn't hesitate.

Master didn't want to die here. Purple witch knows more.

There was a lot to unpack in that. "*Master* as in Aunt Lizzie?" I murmured quietly to Sherlock. It was what he'd called my aunt when I'd first moved to town, but as usual, he didn't answer my outright question.

He may have been right that Marigold knew more, but I wondered how many more times we would have to question her before she revealed all of the many truths she kept a secret from others.

As we drove down the mountain, and the more I thought about Marigold's motives in all of this, unfortunately, the more sense it made.

I spoke my theories aloud. "Marigold has always been after power in this town. She's always been jealous of other witches. Even though she's considered the Queen Witch now, I've always had the feeling it's not enough for her, or that she's trying hard to prove that she's far better than she is. I wonder if she could have thought that Aunt Lizzie's death being a suicide would somehow make my aunt seem weaker in everyone's minds?" I suggested, my best guess.

"It's possible," Jay put in, as he navigated along the bumpy dirt road. "As far as I can understand, Marigold held the title even before Lizzie died, but most of the town felt as though Lizzie was the more genuine leader." That agreed with everything I'd learned about my aunt in the last year. Jay went on. "Perhaps Marigold simply knew Lizzie was going to try the stunt and felt guilty for not stopping her?"

"From the beginning, I had a thought that Marigold had sent herself the death threats. Why had we discounted that idea?"

"You interviewed her and felt she was being forthright." It didn't sound like blame in Jay's tone, but I took it that way.

"Maybe she's just a really good actress." I couldn't shake the feeling that Marigold was somehow involved in this, and my sea glass remained warm to confirm it.

"Maybe she's hiding a whole lot of guilt," Pepper put in.

"Were Marigold and Aunt Lizzie true enemies?" I asked Jay. I'd never completely gotten a handle on how deep or shallow their friendship went.

"Not enemies. Definitely not." He shook his head. "But there were power struggles with Lizzie, with Donna, with a lot of the local witches. Even if those power struggles ran so strong they were lethal, though, Marigold definitely didn't kill Donna herself on Saturday night. There's no way she could have made it out to the lighthouse in order to cut the wire. And, to be honest, I don't know that she has enough favor with anybody in town anymore in order to get them to carry out something like that on her behalf."

I kept thinking about how the death threats looked like Rachael's artwork. Could that have been constructed on purpose in order to blackmail another witch into helping her? My mouth went dry with this thought, as Rachael was always trying to prove her worth in different ways among the witches. I thought she'd been less worried about proving herself to Marigold in recent months, but what if I was wrong?

Then again, Marigold was the one who pointed out the clearly different paint pens that were used on the death threats. Why would she have done that if she was trying to frame Rachael?

As we arrived at the bottom of the mountain, Aaron told Jay to drop him off at the station. "I'll file a report and get forensics up there to make sure we haven't missed anything."

"And I'll let you know if we discover anything new from Marigold Weathers," Jay told him as we arrived at the police station.

Marigold, unfortunately, was with a fortune-telling client when we arrived. She didn't answer her upstairs door, and when we knocked at the downstairs door, she snapped it open, annoyed.

"What do you want?" She looked between us. "I'm with someone?"

"How long do you expect your appointment to be?" Jay asked, crossing his arms, and letting her know with his tall posture that he wasn't about to back down.

"I don't know, another hour? And then I have to rush straight to work at my son's store."

Jay nodded, pulling out his phone. "Finish with your client. I'll make arrangements with your son for you to be a little late." He was already dialing, not leaving any room for her arguments. "We'll be out here when you're done."

It turned out Marigold didn't have to work until four, which was still several hours away.

"So she lied," I whispered to Jay.

"Or at least stretched the truth."

Pepper had plunked down on the grass to pet Sherlock. Oregon was always damp this time of year, but she didn't seem to care, and Sherlock had really taken to Pepper since her arrival. Next time Pepper and I were alone, I planned to ask her if she felt or heard anything special from my cat.

Jay had to make a call into the station to have a short briefing about lab and autopsy reports. While he did that, I went and dropped down on the ground beside Pepper.

Once Jay was out of earshot, she whispered, "What does your sea glass say?"

I touched it, surprised I hadn't thought of checking in with it in the last few hours. When my hand wrapped around it now, there was no real temperature to it. I unclasped it and passed it to Pepper. "I've got nothing. Why don't you check."

She looked happy that I'd trust her with this task.

But less than a minute later, she shook her head and handed it back. "So what does that mean? Is it broken? Or is our connection with it broken? Maybe it's because we've been talking all about it's magic?" Her last word was barely a whisper.

I also had to point out another possibility. "Or maybe Marigold isn't as guilty as we think she is."

Pepper rolled her eyes, and without her even saying it, I knew what she was thinking: That I was too close to the situation. Too close to Marigold.

And maybe she was right. In truth, I couldn't imagine much worse than finding out that someone I know in town here, someone I'd even considered a friend, could have hurt Aunt Lizzie or Donna Davine.

Deep down I didn't think that was true, but at the same time, I didn't discount the fact that Marigold had just lied to us. What were the chances she wasn't covering *something* up?

While we waited for Marigold and Jay paced the backyard with his phone to his ear, I pulled out my spreadsheet app on my phone. I started a new sheet and listed all the possible suspects I'd come up with so far in the first column.

I put Marigold at the top, but along her row I added notes about her being in full view during the entire solstice festival and about her friendship with Donna, which I understood had been intact at the time of Donna's death.

Then I dropped down a line and added Reg Carlson's name. Even though he didn't have a criminal record, I didn't trust the guy, and every time I thought of him, I wanted to figure out a way to convince Olivia to steer clear of him.

Then came Nate Miller, Donna's overprotective boyfriend. I wondered if Officer Grant had updated Jay with any new information about him.

I also included all the witches I knew by name, and descriptions of those I couldn't name. The general motive for any of them was the internal power struggle, but it was still difficult to know if any of them had the means and opportunity to kill on Saturday night. According to Rachael, some of them had alibis, but I hadn't had a chance to ask her yet the names of those she'd crossed off the list, so I kept them all on until I knew more. I added every detail I had on all of what I considered our prime suspects, but my sea glass still sat cool against my collarbone.

Maybe Pepper was right. Had we done something to mess with its magic? It was hard to believe that we were on the wrong track with all of these people.

Or maybe I had to be closer to them to feel a temperature change?

I was still deliberating over this when Marigold opened her door to escort out an elderly lady who I'd seen around town. She didn't frequent the café, so I didn't know her name. Pepper and I stood while Jay hung up his call. Marigold glanced at the three of us, and then decided to walk her client all the way out to her car.

During the wait, we all stared at each other with raised eyebrows. Marigold's avoidance wasn't doing her any favors as far as not appearing guilty of some wrongdoing.

I forced a deep breath and reminded myself that appearances were a lot less important than proof. I was still holding out hope that Marigold would tell us something that would answer all of our questions about both Donna and Lizzie, without having to pin their deaths on anyone I knew.

Pepper was right. I was too close to this.

As Marigold made her way back around the house and toward us, I fisted my hands at my sides, trying to emotionally steel myself so I could be clearheaded about the investigation.

"Now, what's this about?" Marigold crossed her arms. It was cold outside, and we'd already been waiting for her for half an hour in the near-freezing December air, but she didn't invite us inside.

Jay, though, didn't have any problem asking for exactly what he wanted. "Let's go inside and talk, Marigold. We have some new threads of information that have opened up around a recent investigation and we'd like to ask you about them."

"We?" Marigold raised an eyebrow in a way that felt like a sneer. She didn't think Pepper and I should have any part of this, that was clear, and yet Jay led the way to the door, opened it, and motioned for us all to go inside.

I swallowed hard. I hated getting trapped between friendships and investigative work. Jay was so good at that, and I wondered how long it would take me to be more relaxed about it, or if that would ever happen.

Marigold made sure to shut the door before Sherlock got inside. There were only two chairs across an empty table of Marigold's basement—the area I jokingly referred to as fortune-telling central. It was built to be an area that only comfortably fit Marigold and a single client.

Marigold started to pull back a chair to sit, but when she noticed none of us were planning to sit, she tucked the chair back in. "What's this about?"

"I understand you helped Donna prepare for her flying stunt on Saturday night?" He opened his pad of paper to a new sheet.

"Yes, I've already told you that." Marigold sounded annoyed. "And it should have gone off without a hitch. I'm waiting for you to tell me what happened, exactly, because the whole thing should have been flawless." Her voice sounded strong, and yet her gaze flicked away from Jay for just a second, and I sensed something behind it. Guilt?

Jay nodded and made a note. "Can you tell me what type of cable wire was used and where it was purchased?"

She nodded, and started to soften a little in her stance, like she, as well, was about to get some answers. "We employed a local engineer and he told Donna to order three hundred feet of galvanized 7 x 19 inner wire rope core from Happy Hardware. Anything less would have been too dangerous."

Pepper and I looked at each other on her last word, but Marigold didn't seem to notice the irony of her statement and went on.

"This whole thing was not planned without hours and hours of research and test runs and safety precautions in place. This was not my fault!"

Jay nodded, calmly, and made notes of all she said. "Can you tell me when and where you ran test runs for this stunt?"

Marigold's gaze darted away from Jay again, for just a second. "Exactly where she performed it Saturday. Because it was located over the beach, not many would have noticed the wire, but it's been there for two weeks. We dropped it down last Sunday, so it was barely five feet above the water. We were up there each evening, testing the strength, moving it higher and higher each day until it was at full height."

"And did you test it out yourself?" Jay asked, still writing.

"Oh, I would have. I most definitely would have. But my priority was keeping Donna safe, and someone had to be on the ground to make sure the entire apparatus was functioning properly. Plus, I had two witches stationed at the lighthouse and two at the Town Hall. Donna was the one who wanted to do it during the festival, so she was the one I wanted to give the practice time to."

I had trouble not making a face at Marigold's magnanimous sounding words, as did Jay, apparently, but he sucked in his lips to hide his expression and kept writing.

"And how difficult was it to move the height of the wire each evening?"

Marigold now pulled out a chair, either getting more relaxed at this line of questioning, or simply tired of standing. "The nylon round slings were simple to move up and down on either side, but we ended up needing a couple dozen of the screw pin anchors. When I decided to include this event at our festival, I hired the best engineer in town to help us plan it, and in fact, he checked everything over."

"What was the name of this engineer and how did you find him?" Jay asked.

"I went to the Town Hall and they referred me to the city's main engineer, Henry McGill. He's usually busy with work for the city, but then he had a sudden opening, and right in time for our festival. We couldn't have asked for better luck." Marigold blinked and then seemed to realize what she'd said. She looked at the table in front of her.

"So walk me through it. You went to Mr. McGill and asked him to help you rig a tightrope wire over the ocean and he told you what to buy for that?"

Marigold shook her head. "Oh no. I had no idea where to rig the setup. Mr. MgGill suggested trying it near the water, as the lighthouse and the Town Hall were both immovable concrete structures."

"And Mr. McGill was the one who suggested the screw pin anchors to attach the wire at either end?"

Marigold nodded. "And the nylon slings. Thankfully, Happy Hardware was able to get in exactly what was needed in plenty of time."

Had it been in plenty of time? I recalled CJ mentioning he'd had to put a rush on the items.

Something was eating away at me, even though it seemed like Marigold was being more than helpful with an abundance of details. Before Jay launched into his next question, it came to me, and I blurted my own question before I could stop myself.

"So this week was the only time you've practiced a high-wire act? You had never attempted to do it before with any other witches?" Jay had instructed us to leave Lizzie's name out of the questioning until after he got some more information out of her. But it took all my strength not to ask the question I really wanted to ask: Had she tried this stunt with Lizzie?

"After hiring a special engineer, it was our plan to have this as part of our summer and winter solstice festivals for many years to come." I wondered if I had imagined it, or if Marigold's skin had gone paler in the last thirty seconds.

Thankfully, Jay didn't miss the fact that she hadn't answered my question. "To your knowledge, had any of the local witches attempted a flying-type stunt before this last week?"

Her eyes widened—feigned innocence, or true innocence? "Well, I can't speak for all of the local witches, so I'm afraid I wouldn't know."

"If you had to guess..." Jay went on, pressing the issue. "Who do you think would have tried it? Who do you think may have purchased wire from our local hardware store in the past and set up this stunt, perhaps somewhere out of town?"

Now Marigold's face went stark white. My mouth went as dry as a desert and my sea glass heated so hot it felt like it was melting into my skin.

We had her. Marigold had been keeping something very big from us, and it definitely had to do with Aunt Lizzie.

Chapter Nineteen

I LOOKED TO WHERE her stairs led up to the second floor, suddenly recalling something I'd seen when I'd come by for the death threats. "Where's that red bin that was over there the last time I was here?" I pointed.

I never expected anything like what happened next. Marigold let out a loud cry, buried her face in her hands and started sobbing into them.

Jay stood there, as stunned as I was. Pepper didn't know Marigold, and Jay's number one job was to get to the truth and solve the investigation, so I knew it was up to me to stop Marigold from falling completely apart.

I moved beside her and wrapped an arm around her shaking shoulders. If she did have something to do with Aunt Lizzie's death, she was clearly devastated about it.

"Tell us what happened," I told her gently. "We can't help you and we can't tie up the investigation around Donna's death unless we know the truth. All of the truth. Past and present."

She shook her head, her purple hair moving stiffly, like it had too much hairspray in it. "It wasn't the same thing with Donna," she blubbered through her tears. "We had planned it out so carefully, so it wouldn't happen again. We didn't leave a single thing to chance!"

"So what wouldn't happen again?" Jay's voice had dropped quieter, but he still kept his all-business tone. When time stretched on, and she didn't look up from her hands and answer, he eventually added, "Marigold, you need to tell us if this has to do with Lizzie Rose."

At the sound of my aunt's name, Marigold let out a loud wail. We waited her out while she collected herself. Pepper frowned, like she was having a hard time accepting this new insight into our aunt's death. I would have trouble processing it, too, when I had time to really think about it.

Finally, Marigold's cries subsided. "I swear, she was the one who wanted to try it. I didn't talk her into it, I only helped her to prepare."

I couldn't keep my mouth shut. "Were you there? When she fell?"

Marigold shook her head and dropped it into her hands on the table. "I should have been. We were supposed to go up there and try it out as soon as we could get a few witches together to cheer us on. Both of us were going to try it. But then she went ahead on her own."

Jay opened his mouth to ask another question, but I was suddenly overwhelmed by my own questions and I had to know what really happened to Aunt Lizzie. "Why would she do that? Why would she go up on her own?"

Marigold looked down and spoke to the tabletop. "I had the same questions. I didn't know either until I came back to her houseboat and found her note." She glanced over at Jay, but only for a second. "I didn't touch it. I left it where it was for the police to find."

Even after reading it again today, I'd only taken in bits and pieces of what I had believed to be my aunt's suicide note. "What did her note mean to you?" I had to ask.

Jay pulled it up on his phone and read it aloud. "To My Community, My Crystal Cove: Today, I am flying into the Great Beyond. This world has allotted me many friends and many blessings, but it's not enough, not the way it is. I have to do this, today, all on my own. After this, we'll all know. It's my only way to find a better tomorrow. With lasting love, Lizzie."

Now Marigold looked up at me and her face was streaked with tears. "She wanted to fly for the first time at the Friendship Festival. That was the festival she was planning, but I'd first come up with the idea, so I argued that we should save it for the summer solstice festival, which was the one I was planning." Marigold shook her head. "Up until that note, she'd always talked about how *we* would do this together, and rule this town together."

I'd always thought the witchy power struggle in Crystal Cove only went one way, but had Aunt Lizzie been vying for power from Marigold as well?

Jay stepped in. "Someone must have helped Lizzie that day. She wouldn't have been able to get up on the wire on her own."

"I know!" Marigold's eyes went wide. "I've been interrogating every one of the local witches for almost a year, and I still have no idea. Either they are all very good actresses, or they truly knew nothing about Lizzie flying on the wire. When I first suggested the same feat to Donna, and then as we prepared to make it happen, I was certain I would see some guilt on at least one of them, but nothing! They all seemed confused about how the feat would even work."

"Who else, other than the local witches, knew about the high-wire act back when you and Lizzie were planning it?" Jay asked.

She shook her head. "I hadn't told a soul. Lizzie must have told someone, because otherwise, I have no idea."

"What about the cable and other paraphernalia? Were you the one to take that down after she fell?"

Marigold nodded, guiltily. "I knew if the police found all of that, it would come back to me. Lizzie and I had been spending a lot of time on it in the weeks before her death. After I first saw her note, I felt guilty for having pushed her into something she hadn't been ready for. I know I can be a strong personality, hard to approach sometimes. But, worse than my own guilt, I realized that if people truly thought she went up there to prove herself against me, it would be awful for this town, and no one would ever trust any of the witches again. Better to let Lizzie's memory go on as someone selfless, but pained."

My brow creased. Jay went on to ask about details of setting up the cable and taking it down. I tuned most of it out, swept up in my own inner questions until I heard him say, "What do you mean, it snapped up near the tree trunk at the top?"

She nodded. "It made it harder for me to haul away on my own. When Lizzie and I had brought the cable up there, it had taken both of us to carry it. If it had snapped in the middle, I would have been able to handle the two pieces a lot easier, but as it was, I had to use my wheelbarrow."

Jay was furiously making notes. I felt in my bones—and in my hot sea glass—that something was wrong, but I wasn't sure what. "And you said you didn't hire an engineer to help with the stunt back then?"

Marigold shook her head. "I tried, but Mr. McGill was too busy at the time."

Jay marked down Mr. McGill's name and put an asterisk beside it. "And you purchased all the supplies from Happy Hardware?"

Marigold stood and nodded. "I went back to CJ a couple of months after Lizzie's accident and asked if I could return the cable. I said I didn't end up needing it. I figured since most of it was intact, if he didn't measure it, he'd never know that it had been used, and I really needed the money."

"And did he refund you for it?" Jay didn't look up from his furious notes, but I watched Marigold carefully.

Marigold moved to a side wall that was draped by red curtains. I thought it was simply to add to the mystical magical ambiance of her fortune-telling room, but when she swept back one curtain, I was surprised to see shelves of storage, filled to the brim. Many items were in red storage bins, and right away, I spotted the one with the rope, right at the bottom on the far left. But now that it was uncovered and I had more than a second to look at it, I could see it wasn't rope at all, but a huge spool of thick looking cable.

She motioned to it. "He said no one in town would ever use wire like that, and he wouldn't give me a penny for it." As she spoke, Jay moved over and crouched in front of the storage bin. I was glad to have him blocking my view of it, and maybe that was his point. Marigold went on, now speaking to me. "Mr. McGill assured me that this was the weight of cable I needed, and I knew it would have saved Donna a bundle to try and use the same cable again on Saturday night, but I couldn't put anyone else's life in danger. I made Donna try it repeatedly, and at very low heights, so she couldn't possibly be hurt. As I raised the wire each night, I kept watching the other witches, who were all there to help. I watched them for any sign that they'd seen this before or were having trauma flashbacks."

It seemed like Marigold was trying to make herself feel better, feel innocent in all of this, but I could no longer even look at her.

She'd had a hand in my aunt's death, and had been keeping the details to herself all this time.

I didn't know if I'd ever be able to forgive her for that.

Chapter Twenty

We were back in Jay's car before I could speak again. "Marigold has been responsible for Lizzie's death this whole time." She said she was looking for other witches who might have been with Lizzie that day, but I'd been able to see the guilt all over Marigold. She was making a last-ditch effort to direct Jay's attention to anywhere else.

"I'm not so sure about that."

I couldn't believe Jay was defending her. I slumped back into my seat, eyes wide and set straight ahead. Surely, at least Pepper would be on my side about this.

I wasn't planning to say a word to her about it until we were alone at the marina. I couldn't coax a single word out of my mouth as my fury rose within me.

But, surprisingly, Pepper spoke up, sounding about as calm as she ever had. Then again, she had never been close to Aunt Lizzie. "Marigold said the cable split at one side. Were you able to see the side that had the breakage?" Sherlock was curled up on her lap, not saying a word to me about any of this. At least Pepper sounded fully awake now. I wondered if I'd have to take this whole case to Aaron myself, if Jay had been swayed by Marigold's emotional outburst.

Jay glanced in his rearview mirror at my sister. "No. In fact, there was no difference at all between the two ends."

They went on conversing without me. I looked out the passenger window, losing myself in thoughts of Aunt Lizzie, and how she'd trusted Marigold. I wondered if there was any truth to the competitiveness between them for the different festivals, or if Marigold had simply been too scared to try the stunt, so she sent Aunt Lizzie up there first.

"So you believe it had been cut with the same type of battery-powered cutter?" Pepper's question snagged my attention back to their conversation.

"What are you talking about? Marigold actually cut the cable and watched Aunt Lizzie fall?" I sat up straight in my seat, suddenly livid.

But Jay placed a hand on my arm, trying to calm me. "I don't think so, Tabby. I think this was someone else. Perhaps, you were right all along, and the person who had cut the cable while Donna was on it, had cut Lizzie's as well."

I rubbed my forehead. It took me several long seconds to understand what he was telling me. "You think my aunt was murdered?" Sherlock popped his head up off Pepper's lap at this suggestion.

"I still need to prove it," he said, but he was nodding with this revelation.

A second later, I had my spreadsheet pulled up on my phone. Once I had the list of suspects up, Jay leaned over and Pepper leaned up from the backseat as we looked it over.

"Adding Lizzie's death into the mix changes things," Jay said. "Do we have any reason to suspect Nate Miller of having anything against Lizzie and Donna?"

I shook my head slowly. "Not that I know of. How can we find out if Reg Carlson was around town when Lizzie died?"

"I can have a private word with Olivia," Jay suggested. "Marigold certainly seems to believe it was one of the other witches up there with Lizzie."

As I stared at the witches' names on my spreadsheet, my intuition, not to mention my sea glass, told me that wasn't it. I had no real way to explain why. "Maybe we should talk to Rachael again, too, given all of this new information?"

"Good idea," Jay agreed.

I sat back into my seat as we arrived at the marina. I was so stunned, I didn't know if I was even capable of walking back to my aunt's boat. "So we're talking about a serial killer? In Crystal Cove?"

Jay took in a big breath and let it out slowly before answering. "If that's the case, we're looking for someone local, someone who has been here the whole time, living right under our noses with the knowledge that they've killed two women."

As much as that thought sickened me, we were getting closer to the truth. I could feel it.

And if Aunt Lizzie's killer was the same person who had killed Donna Davine, I wouldn't stop searching until I discovered the truth.

# Chapter Twenty-one

ONCE I GOT TO work at the café, I found myself getting every second order wrong and having to remake it. I'd wanted to call in sick and continue to help with the investigation, but Jay assured me he would be at the station briefing the rest of the force this afternoon, and there wasn't much I could do to help with that. Plus, he'd told me it was best to keep my life looking as normal as possible for the moment, and see if I caught wind of any interesting tidbits of information from the patrons at the café.

"This has sugar in it," an older gentleman named Marty who frequented the café told me, passing his mug across the counter to me and taking my attention back from where it had been—on what local person had kept the details of Aunt Lizzie's death a secret for almost a year.

"Oh! I'm so sorry. What was it you wanted?" I looked down and my hands were shaking. He reminded me that it was supposed to be a skim latte with cinnamon, and I repeated his words over and over again as I made up his correct order.

"Maybe you should start writing people's orders down," Marty suggested, as he took his order. It hurt, because since I started working at the café, I'd prided myself on being able to keep orders straight without writing them down, but today my mind was going in too many different directions.

I'd told Pepper she could come into the café and we could put our heads together over the case, but she had another stop to make first. She was taking Sherlock to the beach to try and find herself a piece of sea glass that called to her.

Now that we had a murderer on the loose in Crystal Cove—a person who had most likely killed my aunt as well—I was nothing but eager for my sister to grow in her gifting with magic. I wanted all the help I could get to figure this out.

Between customers, I roamed the café, cleaning tables and eavesdropping on conversations, but I didn't hear anything of interest.

I updated my spreadsheet of suspects on my phone from behind the counter. I couldn't yet take Marigold off of the list, although it seemed Jay felt she wouldn't be strong or agile enough to haul a ladder up to the start of Aunt Lizzie's "flight."

So were we talking about several witches who had conspired to keep the details of Lizzie's death a secret? Or someone else altogether?

I reluctantly moved Donna Davine's overprotective boyfriend, Nate Miller, to the bottom of my list. I hadn't discovered a motive for him in Donna's murder, and I hadn't found any connection to Aunt Lizzie. Plus, the timing wasn't right for him to have had the opportunity to be at the top of the lighthouse during Donna's stunt. I couldn't bring myself to remove him from the list altogether, as I'd still rather think of someone like him as being responsible than one of my witch friends.

Then there was Olivia's ex-boyfriend Reg Carlson. Jay was ignoring the fact that the guilty party didn't have to be a local if it was someone who frequented Crystal Cove—right at the time when there happened to be murders. I didn't trust the guy, and I was even starting to trust Olivia less and less. She'd barely stayed long enough to say hello when I'd shown up at the beginning of my shift today. I wondered if Reg would be with her again when she came to lock up.

Jay had watched the guy's car and the bed and breakfast all night. Reg hadn't gone anywhere or done anything suspicious, but we had nothing to exonerate him from the crime yet, either. I left him near the top of my suspects list, even though I had yet to find a clear motive or opportunity for him. I knew I wasn't being completely rational, but I also couldn't bring myself to remove anyone from my list.

As I began looking through the names of each of the local witches, a young family I recognized but didn't know by name entered the café and walked up to the counter.

The man ordered for all three of them, and this time I wrote their orders down before entering them into the till. "A large chai with whole milk and no sugar, a large mint mocha, and a small hot chocolate please."

As I made up their order, glancing at my list over and over again as I did it to make sure I was getting them right, I tried to decide which drink was for which adult.

Their little blonde girl of no more than five pointed into the bakery display and said, "Look, Mommy! Fireworks!" She was pointing at the cupcakes with multi-colored sprinkles that Olivia had put out this morning.

The mom, also blonde, squatted near her daughter. "They do look like fireworks, don't they?" She sighed and looked up at me as I arrived at the counter with their hot drinks. "I suppose we should get one of those, too."

The little girl clapped her hands, but as the woman stood, her husband murmured, "That's a lot of sugar."

That told me everything I needed to know and I placed the sugarless chai in front of the man. After passing the other drinks out, I rang up their order and then looked at the man in question.

"Shall I add a sprinkle cupcake?"

His wife gave him a pleading look as his daughter turned in circles with her hot chocolate, which I'd purposely made more lukewarm instead of hot, in case she spilled it. The matter seemed already decided in her mind.

He let out a long sigh. "I suppose if this makes her feel like she's seen the fireworks, that might finally get her to stop talking about it."

I added the cupcake to the total, and while the man paid on our debit machine, I dug into the bakery display for the cupcake that had the most sprinkles. As I packed it into a small box for the girl, the woman explained the situation to me, as though she, too, now felt guilty for feeding her daughter so much sugar.

"Carly had been so looking forward to seeing the fireworks at the solstice festival the other night. She's never seen fireworks before, so we promised she could stay up late that one night to see them. But of course after that awful tragedy, they never ended up happening."

As she said this, I vaguely remembered hearing rumors of fireworks that were supposed to end the solstice festival. I guess I'd gotten it in my head that the flying stunt had taken their place as the big event instead. It had certainly felt that way, especially when the stunt turned deadly.

"Where were the fireworks supposed to go off?" I asked, reining the family back after they'd already turned to leave.

The woman turned back. "I don't know for sure, but every time we've had fireworks in Crystal Cove in the past, they've lit them out in the water on the recycling barge."

A barge? We hadn't considered that. Crystal Cove did keep an ever-present barge not far off shore. Recycling was stored there until it was full and then disappeared for a day or two to unload somewhere.

But before I could ask the family anything else about the barge or the expected fireworks, they hurried out the door after their sugar-energized little girl.

Chapter Twenty-two

I HAD MY PHONE to my ear and it was already ringing when Pepper finally came through the door to the café.

Jay answered as she arrived at the counter, so I held up a finger to her, but moved close enough that she would hear, too. As I did, I saw the small oval piece of pink sea glass she held in her palm. Pink sea glass is one of the rarest colors. I was surprised she'd found such a nice shade and in such a perfect oval. That, in itself, had to be magic.

"Tabby, I was just about to call you to check in," Jay said on the other end.

We still had customers all around, so I couldn't put it on speakerphone, but I hoped Pepper would get most of the updates from hearing my end of the conversation. "I'm glad I got a hold of you. I just had a family in here, and they were talking about fireworks at the solstice festival. Do you know anything about that, or can you find anything out?"

"There were fireworks planned for Saturday night?" Jay confirmed. "Huh."

When he didn't immediately see the relevance, I realized I hadn't told him the most important part. "I've heard fireworks are often out on the recycling barge, and well, we never thought of someone reaching the reef unnoticed from the barge, did we?"

"Huh," he said again, but this time the one word held a lot more interest. Then he murmured to someone in the background. When he came back on the line, he said, "If they had planned fireworks, they would have had to have pulled a permit from the Town Hall for it. I'll look into who had access to the recycling barge."

"Do you know if the barge was definitely anchored off shore on Saturday night?"

"It's more than possible," Jay said, his words suddenly hurried. "And you're right, that would've given someone an opportunity to get out to the reef without being noticed from the mainland. I'm going to look into this myself. If I can get some information at the Town Hall before it closes, I'll be by right after to let you know what I discover."

He hung up quickly after that. Pepper, smart girl that she was, had put most of it together.

"There might have been a barge out past the reef, and that's where the murderer may have come from?" she guessed in a whisper. She rubbed her sea glass as she made this assumption.

I nodded and motioned to it. "You found a piece that called to you? Did you know that pink is the rarest color of sea glass?"

"Really?" Her eyes lit up and she held it up, as if to try and look through it. "I wasn't sure, until you mentioned the barge. Then it got warm between my fingers."

"Who would have been running the fireworks for the witches' festival? The local fire department?" Unfortunately, I didn't know any of the local firemen. I looked to the rear of the café at the next best thing. Marigold hadn't been in since the festival, but plenty of other witches had been filling the place, always leaned in to one another whispering. I had plenty to ask them now. I figured I should wait on many of the integral questions surrounding Aunt Lizzie's death, but at the very least, I could find out if any of them knew who was in charge of the fireworks for Saturday night.

"Do you know anyone you can ask?" Pepper said, not noticing my gaze. "Maybe Marigold?"

That would be my last choice. Rachael would be my first choice, but Aaron had mentioned earlier how busy she was with housecleaning jobs today. Best to start with someone else, someone right here in the café, who might know more about the planned fireworks display.

"Want to come behind the counter and wash your hands? I have an idea."

Pepper didn't hesitate, and five minutes later, we had a tray filled with cut up samples from the bakery display. Olivia was all for giving free refills in order to get people to stay and buy bakery items, but my suggestion of actually offering samples of the bakery items had so far been met with a headshake. So I slipped a twenty-dollar bill from my own purse into the till to cover it, and headed out to the café seating, leaving Pepper to greet customers from the counter in my absence. I started with the back upper level of the café, where the witches usually hung out.

Today, there were six of them. They'd pulled their tables together and, as usual, were whispering across them. The two I knew by name happened to be sitting together, so I headed for that end of the tables.

"Sheena, Ruth? Would you like to try a sample from the bakery display?"

They shook their heads without looking up at me. Shoot. Maybe this wouldn't work after all, if they were so involved in their private conversation that even tasty treats wouldn't pull their attention away.

Before I'd figured out another angle, one of the witches across the table piped up. "I'll try one. Are those blueberries I see?"

I grinned and rounded the table toward her. "You bet." I turned my tray so she could retrieve the one she wanted.

"Olivia's blueberry lavender coffee cake is a favorite here at The Heirloom Café."

She helped herself to one.

"Would anyone else like to try something? I also have pumpkin spice muffin samples and fruit explosion cupcakes." I motioned to the cupcake with sprinkles I'd cut up. "Funny thing, a little girl came in the café earlier and told her mom the sprinkles looked like fireworks." My sea glass warmed as the segue came to me in an instant. "Apparently, she'd been looking forward to seeing fireworks for the first time on Saturday at the festival. I hadn't been aware any fireworks were in the plans."

Other witches were stuck on my descriptions of the baked goods and were helping themselves, but Ruth and Sheena now stared at me with their jaws set as though they didn't appreciate me asking questions regarding the festival.

Too bad, because all the other witches at the table suddenly seemed to like having me around. As one with orange hair twice as bright as mine helped herself to the pumpkin spice muffin quarter, she told me, "If not for the horrible tragedy, Saturday night would have ended in fireworks."

"Is that right?" I kept my gaze on her. "I hear they usually set them off from a barge in the water. I imagine that would be quite a spectacular sight."

The orange-haired witch's eyes turned sad as she nodded.

"You didn't see the fireworks on the Fourth of July?" Ruth asked, her tone curt. The brashness I felt off of Ruth and Sheena made me feel as though I should be investigating *them* closer regarding Donna's death. I'd seen Sheena serving up candy apples at one of the vendor booths Saturday night, but I didn't recall seeing Ruth. What if Ruth and another witch had been overseeing the fireworks on the barge, in order to use their position to get to the reef and cut the wire? What if Marigold had been lying and had orchestrated the whole thing, or had simply been too close to the situation to see the guilt in her witch friends?

I shook off all these thoughts for the moment, in order to answer. "I heard the Fourth of July fireworks, but I'd been dealing with a burst pipe on one of the houseboats that night." Truth be told, I'd never been a huge fan of fireworks. In Portland, fireworks always equaled huge and usually disrespectful crowds. It was how I'd come to equate them, but I felt like I was doing a pretty good job of playing up my supposed love of them. "It must be quite an ordeal, to get them all setup on a barge out in the water. And a huge expense, too. I hope your group isn't out too much money, considering they didn't even end up getting used."

"Oh no," the orange-haired witch answered me before a sharp shush out of Ruth made it across the table to her.

We all looked to Ruth, but Ruth's gaze was trained on the orange-haired witch. Her voice was quiet and low when she said, "You know what Marigold told us about Donna's death being no accident. She works with the police!" The last word came out as almost a hiss.

Even though the statement wasn't directed at me, I decided to respond to it. "It's true, I do help out with investigations from time to time, but rest assured, Detective Jameson has been working very closely with Marigold Weathers on anything related to Saturday night's tragedy." If it was simply a case of the local witches looking out for one another, I could at least help them relax in that regard. "He has her full support." Sure, we'd pretty much needed to trap her in her lies in order to get that support, but it wasn't a lie.

Ruth stared at me for a moment, assessing my honesty, but then answered. "The Town Hall was kind enough to have taken care of the fireworks for us. We hadn't even considered fireworks, because of the cost, but when we first suggested our itinerary for the festival to the Town Hall, they offered to provide that part themselves."

"Out of the town's funds?" I asked, eyebrows raised.

"I heard the mayor himself offered to pay for them," the orange-haired witch said.

The mayor offered to pay for the fireworks? "Was the mayor out on the barge, ready to set them off?" As I said the words, I recalled that he had been up on the stage not long before Donna's tragic fall.

Besides, was I really about to blame the town mayor for a local murder?

This at least gave me something to discuss with Pepper. We could put our heads together—and our sea glass—and try to figure out where to look for our next move.

Chapter Twenty-three

WHEN I RETURNED TO the counter, Pepper was eager to hear what I'd discovered.

I took in a long breath as I prepared to explain, still barely believing what I'd learned. "Apparently, the mayor had sprung for the fireworks for the solstice festival."

Her eyes widened. "Your mayor may be the killer?" Her words were a quiet whisper.

I shook my head. "He was on the stage, opening the festival, remember?" She looked up, pursing her lips. She'd been so new to town that she likely didn't recall much of anyone. "Besides, it would be especially hard to believe, given that he let the witches use his mansion for the haunted house each year, and by all accounts it seemed he and Lizzie had gotten along well before her death."

"Huh." Pepper said. "I still think he bears investigating. Mark him down on your spreadsheet, and if I were you, I'd send Jay a text right away to let him know."

As soon as I finished doing both of those things, I looked up to see Katie walking through the door.

"Olivia's not here, is she?" she asked in a hushed tone as she made her way to the counter.

I shook my head. "She'll be in in another hour or so to close up."

Katie nodded. "Good. I'm just here for my paycheck." She rounded the counter barrier and headed straight for the till.

Our checks were usually stored under the cash tray and she found hers quickly.

But my concern was why she didn't want to run into Olivia. "What's going on, Katie? It sounds like you're really trying to avoid Olivia."

She shrugged. "I think you should ask her. She took me off the schedule for this week, and I think it's because of that new boyfriend of hers."

"You do?" I glanced to Pepper.

"Yeah, I don't know. Remember how I told you about the guy taking measurements outside the café on Saturday?"

I nodded, vaguely recalling that.

"When she came in to close that night, with him trailing behind her, seeing him jarred my memory. I asked why he'd been taking measurements. He said he hadn't, but I could swear it was the same guy. Then Olivia introduced him as her boyfriend and I got a super weird vibe off the guy. I tried asking Olivia all about him and how long she'd known him and stuff, and next thing I knew, she cut me off and told me that things were slow, so she wouldn't need me this week. I know I can shoot my mouth off sometimes, and I can get in people's business too much, and I tried to tell her that, but she cut me off, not letting me apologize. Then she practically kicked me out, saying she had to close up quickly."

"Didn't you say the guy taking measurements had worn a baseball cap?"

She nodded, getting where I was going with this. "You're right, I can't be positive, but it was his sudden gruffness with me that made me think I was right. Plus, he was still in a dark suit when he came in with Olivia, just without the cap."

Katie didn't deserve to have her hours cut, but more concerning was the fact that Olivia and Reg had both said Reg hadn't arrived in town until late Saturday night. After the murder.

"Do you know anything else about this guy, Reg?" I asked her.

"Not really. I mean, I guess I overheard them talking about where he could rent a boat and how well Olivia knew Frank from the marina. That doesn't mean anything, does it?"

A boat, that could have taken him out to the reef? Or out to the barge to wait until no one was looking? Could he have had anything to do with the fireworks? What if he was somehow connected to Mayor Kelsey? At the very least, it was suspicious that he may have lied about his time of arrival in Crystal Cove.

"It could be important," I told her. "What time did Olivia return to lock up that night?"

"Around eight. My parents were happy they could get to bed early."

Eight would still have been before Donna had fallen to her death, which means Reg definitely lied about the time of his arrival in Crystal Cove.

"Thanks, Katie. Detective Jameson is working on a case right now and this man may be a suspect in it, so if you think of anything else at all that you remember about the guy, will you let me know?

She agreed, and then I told her she'd better get out of here soon if she didn't want to run into Olivia, and possibly Reg.

Olivia returned just before ten, as usual. The café had been quiet for the last hour, and so Pepper and I had discussed the case from every angle we could think of. I hadn't heard back from Jay, which I had to guess meant that he was either too busy to call or he hadn't yet discovered anything new.

I'd thought Olivia was alone, but as Pepper and I headed out the door for the night, I saw a dark Buick across the street with Reg Carlson pacing in front of it with a cell phone to his ear. He was parked near the end of the block. I had an idea and led Pepper down the street away from him and then across to the other side.

"Where are we—?" she started, when she realized I wasn't leading her straight back to the marina.

I held up a hand and our sisterly telepathic connection kicked in without me having to say a word. Two minutes later, I led her around the block, not far from where Reg was parked, but around the corner and out of view.

Thankfully, Reg didn't think anyone was out on the street within earshot, so his voice was loud and easy to hear. "Nope, she's still not willing to sell the place, but don't worry, I'm working on a different angle to get it. Just don't rush in making any offers quite yet."

Didn't Jay say that Reg Carlson's business was transport of some kind? His conversation made me think he might be a realtor or a land developer, at least on the side. After a long minute, he responded to the person on the other end of the line.

"I can't tell you yet, but let's just say if I can work it, it might involve throwing together an impromptu wedding."

My brow crinkled, aimed across the street, where I could barely make out Olivia, flipping chairs up onto tables. Was he serious?

"Oh, don't you worry. It won't be anything permanent. I'll be a bachelor again within a month."

I looked to Pepper and her wide eyes might as well have been a mirror.

Reg Carlson was in town to marry Olivia and scam her out of her café?

Not on my watch. I'd have to find a way to stop his plans, and quickly.

Chapter Twenty-four

BEFORE WE COULD COME up with any way to stop Reg, Olivia headed outside and locked up the café. We ducked further around the corner so we wouldn't be seen, but we could hear Olivia when she said, "Did you get a hold of your business partner?"

"Nah, he wasn't home," Reg said. "I just figured you'd get your closing work done quicker without me distracting you." This comment was filled with innuendo.

I shot Pepper a worried look. Clearly, they were back together. Last time he'd been in town, he'd asked Olivia to sell her place and move to Eugene with him. I'd thought he was chauvinistic for automatically expecting her to be the one to give up her life, but his phone conversation from moments ago gave me a new understanding.

He didn't care where Olivia moved or didn't move. He cared about taking over ownership of the café.

I just didn't understand why.

Moments later, they drove off in his car. We ducked farther out of sight, and I tried to come up with a plan to get her away from him so I could share with her what we'd heard. She'd have to hear me out.

Except...I had a strong suspicion she wouldn't. Olivia was often set in her ways. If she'd decided Reg was a good guy, someone she might even want to marry and start a life with, I suspected it would take more than an eavesdropped conversation to change her mind.

When Reg's taillights disappeared from view, we started back for the marina.

"I'll bet you anything, she's taking him back to her place." I seethed out the words.

Pepper nodded, and it sickened me that she hadn't come up with a disagreement to this. "Is the café really worth a lot? I thought you said Oregon real estate had taken a dive lately."

"It has," I said, still searching for another reasoning for this. "I have to wonder if he was only after her place the last time they were involved, too." If only Donna was still around. I'd love to ask her what, exactly, she'd had against Reg Carlson, because I had a sneaking suspicion it figured closely into his plans now. "Do you think he knew Aunt Lizzie?"

"You'd know better than I would," Pepper told me.

Even though I'd known Aunt Lizzie better than Pepper, I still hadn't seen my aunt in a decade. I didn't know anything. "Could Reg Carlson have been running the fireworks out on the barge?" I asked.

"It's possible, but you said he's not even from here, right?"

"True, but it sounds as though he used to come to Crystal Cove often enough that he likely made some friends, or at least knew some people." I pulled out my phone and dialed Jay, too anxious for answers to wait any longer.

"I wonder if Jay could figure out who he was talking to on the phone," Pepper suggested as the line started to ring.

I automatically put it on speakerphone as it rang again. "He'd need a warrant for that, and to get a warrant, he'd need probable cause for a serious crime. Not just for tricking someone into marrying him for ownership purposes, or lying about what time he arrived in town." The more I got to know Jay, the more I was learning about the law.

One more ring, and finally Jay picked up. "I was just about to call you."

"I hope that means you have news?" My words were so quick, they were almost on top of his.

But during the pause that followed, I could sense him shaking his head. "Unfortunately, no. I got to the Town Hall before it closed, but was given quite the runaround about who had been in charge of the fireworks on Saturday night."

"Avoidance?" I asked. Jay had taught me that this was often an indication of guilt.

"Or just disorganization. Honestly, because it was the end of the day and people were half-packed up to go home, it was a little hard to tell. Some departments had closed early before I got there, so I wasn't able to even figure out which department had headed it up."

"Is there any way Reg Carlson could have been involved?" I asked.

"If they were put on by the Town Hall or the Mayor's Office? Not likely. I know you have a bad feeling about the guy, Tabby, but you might be reaching here."

I shook my head. "It's not just a bad feeling anymore." I explained to him everything we had overheard. "If he lied about when he'd arrived in town, and if he wanted to buy the café when he was dating Olivia before, and if that was Donna's point of contention with him, if he's here to try and trick her into signing ownership over to him again, it would certainly give him a strong motive, at least against Donna."

"That's a lot of if's, Tabby." Jay sighed, and I sensed his frustration in it. "Given Lizzie's death and so much evidence pointing toward the witches, I'm not sure we should be focused on Reg Carlson, just because he's trying to cheat Olivia out of the café and Donna mistrusted him. Which of the witches, if any, benefited from both Lizzie and Donna's deaths? That's what Aaron and I have been trying to figure out. Right now the investigation is going in three different directions: the witches, the fireworks barge, and Reg, and none of them are anywhere near airtight." He took a breath and sighed, while I fought the despondency that tried to overtake me. "Listen," Jay went on. "It's only a dozen hours until the Town Hall opens again in the morning. Are you and your sister free to help me poke around there just after nine?"

"You bet," I told him, checking in on Pepper and recognizing the eager look on her face. "But, Jay. I can't stop thinking about Olivia. I feel like she's taken Reg home with her tonight, and even without airtight proof, what if he's really a murderer?"

"I'll drive by her place and hang out until I can get another officer to come out and take over. I can't drag him out of there without cause, but I can certainly keep an eye on her place for any kind of strange activity."

I felt bad. Jay already had too much work for one person. He often worked late nights and early mornings. "Pepper and I could do it." I looked over at Pepper, and she nodded.

"You're afraid of Olivia being alone with a murderer, and you think I'm going to let *you* go and stakeout the place on your own?" He said with a humorless laugh.

I considered opening my mouth to tell him that if I hadn't brought this to his attention in the first place, we could have simply driven over to Olivia's with or without his permission. But I caught myself before saying anything. This was only a matter of both of us being concerned for the other.

"At least let us come along then?" I asked him.

He sighed and then said, "I'll pick you up in ten."

Chapter Twenty-five

BACK AT THE HOUSEBOAT, Pepper headed straight for the upper deck, grabbing her fuzzy pajamas and slipping into them. She also snatched a blanket from the bed, as though she was fully expecting to spend our entire stakeout sleeping in the car.

I considered suggesting she just stay here, but then what if Jay and I got too tired to keep our eyes open? It would be nice to have her there as a stand-in, in case we needed her.

On that note, I grabbed for Sherlock on our way out the door.

Jay was in the marina parking lot with his engine idling by the time Pepper, Sherlock, and I made it out to him. Pepper automatically took the backseat with her blanket and a fluffy pillow from my aunt's bed, while I took the passenger seat with Sherlock.

Jay was on the phone. "Yeah, okay. No worries. Just thought I'd check." He hung up and looked over at me. "Haven't found anyone to take over for us yet. I've left lots of messages, so maybe someone will get back to me."

He got on the road. I'd only been to Olivia's house once since moving to Crystal Cove. She'd been under the weather one morning, so I'd picked up her café keys to open up. She had said she felt better by the afternoon, although she still looked quite a mess when she came into the café to take over. I'd tried to tell her that I could work, even for free, because she looked like she needed some rest, but she'd insisted she was fine to take care of her own business.

It was the way she was. Responsible and independent. Maybe too much so. I'd always tried to be responsible and independent, like Olivia, back when I lived in Portland, but since moving here I'd been learning the importance of being vulnerable and letting others help me. In addition, I'd learned how to help many of them.

Jay was following the directions of his GPS, but because I knew the house, I pointed as soon as we turned down her street. "It's that brick one, four houses down," I said quickly, so he wouldn't get too close and give ourselves away.

He pulled over to the curb, and may gaze stayed steady on the house while Jay looked back and forth between it and the address on his GPS.

There was no sedan in the driveway. Only Olivia's little smart car.

"Maybe she's staying with him at the bed and breakfast?" I suggested.

Pepper leaned forward between the seats. "But look. There's movement inside, and lights."

Pepper was right. All three of us studied the shadows within the house until we could be sure it was definitely Olivia. It looked as though she was alone.

I turned to Jay. "So he just dropped her off?"

He shrugged and then put his car into gear. "It looks that way, but let's go check the bed and breakfast just to make sure."

Crystal Cove's one bed and breakfast was on the other side of town. It had four guest rooms, which were usually booked up in advance, and it wasn't difficult to make out Reg Carlson's dark sedan right out front.

"What does this mean?" I asked myself more than anyone else. I didn't think it meant we should take him off of our suspect list, but it didn't look like Olivia was in any immediate danger from him.

Were we back to having the other witches as our prime suspects? Or was he simply giving Olivia some space before he proposed?

Jay sighed. "It means we should get some sleep. Get our heads on straight for tomorrow's interviews at the Town Hall. If anyone there knows Reg Carlson or has worked with him in any capacity, then maybe we'll have something to go on in pursuing him as a suspect. I think our best hope is to find something solid about who was on the barge for the fireworks on Saturday night, otherwise we're just going to continue speculating."

I didn't like it. I'd steeled myself for being up on a stakeout all night and my brain was wired for work. I didn't have a clue how I'd get to sleep.

Besides, how did we know for sure Reg wouldn't get up in the middle of the night and head back to Olivia's house to hurt her, or worse?

Before that thought had fully formed, a dozen rebuttals came into my mind about how it would have been easier to cover his tracks if he had gone straight to Olivia's house, if he had any intention of hurting her. As it got later, it was unlikely he could sneak out of the bed and breakfast with no one hearing him. It didn't make sense for him to be back here if he truly intended harm to her, at least for tonight.

I toyed with my sea glass, but it remained cool around my neck.

"Yeah, okay," I finally conceded. "Let's go and get some sleep."

Chapter Twenty-six

THE NEXT MORNING, WHEN I was brewing a pot of coffee, Pepper came down the stairs fiddling with her sea glass, which I had mounted and strung on a chain for her the night before. "I don't know if I'm getting any sense at all anymore. I mean, maybe the other day your intuition was just rubbing off on me. Maybe I don't have any magical abilities."

I shook my head as I pulled out a couple of day-old muffins for us. "I haven't been sensing anything either. All I can think of is that we're either both losing our magic, or we're on the wrong trail."

Pepper slumped into the loveseat beside Sherlock and stroked his fur. I had wanted to ask her more than once if she could communicate with my cat, but the more I thought about it, the more I figured I would have noticed a lot of long strange pauses of her staring at him if that were the case. Besides, when I'd first moved in, Sherlock had told me in his mind-speak that Aunt Lizzie had indicated the new master of the *Lady of Fortune* would be his talking companion. And that was me.

"What if it's because I'm here? What if that's why you're not getting any more intuition?"

As she said the words, I touched my own sea glass. It gave me a pulse of warmth, as though it was letting me know it was still there, it was still working. And a second later, Pepper reached for her own neck. Then she closed her eyes, as if savoring the feeling. It was a far cry from how I'd expected any of my family members to accept our family gift of magic.

Then it occurred to me: "You're up early. And I didn't even have to wake you."

She opened her eyes and raised an eyebrow, still fiddling with her sea glass. "I suppose that is a kind of magic, isn't it?"

"Even without the magic, I've been learning how much I truly can lean on my intuition." I pulled the muffins from my toaster oven and delivered one to Pepper on a plate. "I think part of what I've been learning about Crystal Cove's magic is that it's supposed to be there to enhance the person you already are, not replace it."

I sat at the table with my own muffin, and when Pepper saw me navigating back to my spreadsheet on my phone, she moved over there to join me.

"I figure between my organizational skills and your diagnostic skills, we should be able to sift through the evidence and see what we've been missing. We don't have to rely on either of our magic."

Pepper pulled her chair next to mine so we could both read from my phone screen as we ate. "I keep thinking that all the evidence pointing toward the witches could easily have been someone trying to frame them, especially because the death threats were clearly aimed at framing Rachael."

It was a relief to hear Pepper say this, as I couldn't always depend on myself to be impartial where my friends were concerned.

"So if they were being framed, who would do that, and why?" Pepper tapped her fingers on her sea glass as she chewed her last bite of muffin.

"It seems to me, the deaths of Aunt Lizzie and Donna, and the public disgracing of Marigold, these all led to the witches losing favor with the people in town."

"Who would benefit from the witches losing their power?" Pepper asked. "Who would want to take them down a notch? Do we know Reg Carlson's outlook toward the witches? Maybe it wasn't just Donna he had contentions with?"

Eagerness rose up in me from this theory. "Maybe he wants to buy Olivia's café so he can establish himself in Crystal Cove and accumulate his own power?" I touched my sea glass, but it remained cool.

Pepper watched me and turned thoughtful. "You know something weird about when I had the blue crystal in my purse?"

I leaned in. "What is it?" I'd been restless to learn anything at all about how that blue crystal worked. I knew in my bones it could help me—help make Crystal Cove a better, safer place—but only if I understood how to wield its magic.

"I saw bursts of color. Like while I was walking to the café, it felt as though the red stop light was exploding before my eyes. Do you think it was a warning? Like for us to stop going in the direction we were headed?"

"Could be." I wished we had brought the crystal home from the café with us, so we could search for more insight. Then another sudden idea hit me. "Or did it look more like fireworks?"

As soon as I said the word, my sea glass warmed. Pepper's eyes lit up, with what looked like a new revelation in them.

"One way or another, we need to find out who was responsible for setting up the fireworks on the barge Saturday night," I said.

"And if it wasn't Reg Carlson..." She fingered her own sea glass, which I suspected was also warm. "Who was it?"

Chapter Twenty-Seven

THANKFULLY, JAY KNEW HIS way around the Town Hall. He led the way through the lower doors, down a hallway, through another door, and up to a reception desk. Pepper and I followed, both with a hand on our sea glass. We'd had to leave Sherlock outside, but he seemed happy to sniff around the outer stairs again for clues.

"Hi, Cindy." Jay walked up to the curly-haired receptionist. She was pretty and not much older than me, and I felt a small pang of jealousy when her face morphed into a bright smile at the sight of Jay.

"What can I help you with, Jay?" She sounded like she would help him with pretty much anything he wanted.

Jay glanced back at us before saying, "We just had a few questions about some planned fireworks for last Saturday night. I was in to ask yesterday, and I understand your department handles that, but I guess I got here too late, as you had already left for the day."

Her smile faltered when she realized Pepper and I were with him. "Oh, yes. My nephew had a Christmas concert at his school and my sister really didn't want me to miss it."

I got the feeling in this small town that it wasn't unusual for people to leave their jobs early for family commitments such as this one; however, a police officer bringing it up certainly seemed to bring on some guilt for this woman. Thankfully, Jay knew how to put her mind at ease and get her back on the subject.

He grinned. "Tis the season, isn't it? It seemed most departments had closed by the time I arrived yesterday, so I wasn't able to find out who to check with about those fireworks."

"Oh, right, yes." Cindy moved along her counter so she could peruse a computer screen. She moved her mouse and clicked several times before looking back at Jay. "Fireworks proposals are usually submitted by the Festivals and Planning Committee. I don't see a submission form here. You might want to check with the committee yourself, if there's anyone there today." She chuckled lightly, clearly not understanding the severity of the topic. "They could be off for the holidays already, but you never know. They work on the upper floor, in the same office as Bylaw Enforcement."

She pointed, but before we left, I spoke up with a question of my own as it came to me. "And who does the Festival and Planning Committee usually submit their fireworks proposals to?" My voice had a tinge of desperation to it. I already couldn't stand the fact that the office we needed could be closed until after the holidays.

Cindy looked at me, and her smile faded completely as she took on a business-like tone. "They would normally submit it to us."

I felt my hope deflate.

"Is there any reason the Mayor's Office might have submitted the proposal?" Jay asked, which reminded me that the witches had suggested the Mayor himself had taken on the responsibility of the fireworks.

But Cindy's face stretched in surprise, and she said, "I don't think so."

"Because we heard something about the Mayor arranging them," Jay went on, as if she hadn't spoken.

She chuckled. "People often confuse our infrastructure with the mayor himself. Our organization of town affairs is getting more and more sophisticated every year, and now we have a whole handful of different departments to make sure everything runs efficiently. The Festivals and Planning Committee is what you want."

I thanked her, but she was done looking at me.

"You've been more than helpful, Cindy," Jay said in a warm voice, as Pepper and I backed out of her office. We let him take a few moments to smooth things over with her, in case we needed further help, and then he joined us at the large open staircase leading to the upper floor.

The Bylaw Enforcement Office was easy to find, but nearly empty. Jay also knew the one guy who seemed to be holding down the fort by his first name and asked Jerry if he knew anything about the Festivals and Planning Committee.

"Sherry runs that." The heavyset man motioned to an empty desk near the window. "I think she'll be back in around the twenty-eighth to plan something for New Year's Eve."

"Sherry Morgan?" At Jerry's nod, Jay made a note. I hoped the fact that Jay knew her might mean we could track her down at home. "And had you heard anything about her submitting any fireworks proposals?"

Jerry ran a hand over his jaw as he thought about this. "I couldn't tell you for sure, but I thought I overheard something about no money in the budget for New Year's Eve fireworks."

"I'm not talking about New Year's Eve," Jay told him. "I was wondering about the recent solstice festival. I heard they were supposed to have fireworks."

Jerry shook his head, settling back into his desk chair as though he had work to do. "Not that I know about. Sherry was sure frustrated over the lack of funds, as she said something about the community having come to expect a big bright splash on New Year's Eve."

Jay made another note and thanked Jerry for his help.

As we left his office, I had to wonder if we'd had it wrong all along—If there hadn't been any fireworks planned for Saturday night, and if we'd been chasing a rabbit trail.

But this thought brought on other ideas: Anybody could have been out on the water on a barge or a boat out of sight Saturday night, and if they'd been patient, they would have been able to remain inconspicuous. Reg Carlson could have been out there, and I still hadn't heard back from a nonchalant check-in text I'd sent Olivia first thing this morning.

Chapter Twenty-eight

As we left the Bylaw Enforcement Office feeling discouraged, Jay pointed across the hall. "Let's follow up with the Mayor's Office, just to make sure they don't have any paperwork about it there."

Pepper had her hand on her sea glass and said, "I feel like I should check on Sherlock. I'll be back up in a minute."

She darted down the stairs, and I was left feeling torn. Shouldn't I have been the one taking care of my cat? Shouldn't I have been the one getting a magical inkling about the necessity of doing so?

What if she was right and something was wrong with Sherlock?

But as if he didn't notice my inner turmoil, Jay moved ahead toward the door to the Mayor's Office, expecting me to follow.

The mayor's receptionist, an attractive lady in her fifties, told us Mayor Kelsey wouldn't be in until this afternoon.

So another dead end.

I was still hovering in the doorway, turning to go, when Jay placed his hands on the receptionist's desk and said, "Maybe you can help me, Ginny." She looked up at him in confusion, like she had no idea how she could be of help, so he went on. "It's to do with a case, and time is of the essence on this one."

She nodded, looking up at him with serious eyes. "If I can help, I certainly will."

"We caught wind that there were supposed to be fireworks this past

Saturday night, and we understand they hadn't been arranged through the usual channels of the Festivals and Planning Committee. Can you check and see if they were arranged directly through the Mayor's Office?"

"Our office? Oh, I'm certain they weren't." A crinkle formed between her eyes. "I had heard about fireworks, too, but the witches must have been arranging them and put in for a permit."

I twisted my lips, wondering if this lady was lying, or if the witches had been.

"You're certain they hadn't been directly arranged by the Mayor's Office?" Jay asked.

Ginny looked like she found this idea entertaining, but then her smile quickly flattened when she seemed to remember this was part of an investigation. "Oh, no. Mayor Herschel might have done something like that when he was in office, but no way would

Mayor Kelsey have been that helpful to one of the witch festivals."

"No?" Jay asked. He let the silence fill the air for as long as he had to, until he got an answer.

Ginny felt the discomfort of the moment, clearly, because she started navigating around on her computer screen as she lowered her voice and spoke. "I probably shouldn't be saying this, but Mayor Kelsey has been making things difficult at every turn for those witches since he's taken office. He doesn't like their power over this town, and if you ask me, he's trying to drive them all away."

My mouth went dry at her words. Pepper and I had been looking for someone with a motive to de-power the witches, and we were suddenly aware of Mayor Kelsey's hot and cold changes in attitude toward the local witches. He'd been posing for chummy photos with them around his last election, and apparently during this election, he'd been not only distancing himself from them, he'd possibly been trying to drive them out of town. However, we'd also already established that Mayor Kelsey could not have been out on the reef, as he'd been speaking on the stage at the festival not long before Donna's fall.

Ginny went on about the witches. "They had to submit three proposals for their festival before the Mayor finally approved one—" She stopped suddenly, tilting her head at her computer. "This is strange."

Without asking permission, Jay rounded Ginny's desk. "What's strange?" I moved fully inside the reception office.

She pointed to her screen. "I see the final approval for the solstice festival at the water's edge, right here, and it was signed off on by Mayor Kelsey."

"Yes?" Jay drew out the word, because none of us had thought they were holding the festival without a permit.

"But I think you're right. Those witches must have somehow swayed him, because there's a section here about fireworks, and the whole thing, including the expenses incurred by the engineering department, were filed under billing code 850." She looked up and could quickly tell we had no idea what this meant. "It means the bill wasn't being sent out to the witches or rerouted to the Festivals and Planning Committee. 850 is an expense code. It's what we use when someone threatens to send a nasty opinion piece to the local paper and we have to smooth things over, or when road construction is poorly planned and has to be rerouted." Her confused scowl deepened as she looked closer at her screen. "It's usually used when our office needs to keep something quiet."

It made some sense, if Mayor Kelsey hadn't wanted to be associated with the witches. But then why had Marigold thought of him as so supportive? Why had Mayor Kelsey's engineer suddenly had time to set up the stunt for the witches?

And why hadn't his own receptionist heard about this secret expense?

We all discussed these things down by Jay's car. By this time, Pepper had found Sherlock and had him in her arms. He was no worse for wear, and so I suspected she hadn't quite gotten the hang of the sea glass intuition yet.

"Should we come back this afternoon to question Mayor Kelsey?" I asked. I still couldn't believe our local mayor could have somehow been involved in cold-blooded murder. Not to mention, unless he had some really powerful magic of his own, he wouldn't have been able to be in two places at once.

Jay nodded. "That certainly seems like our next step."

I pulled out my phone and brought up Katie's contact. While Jay filled Pepper in about everything else we had learned from the mayor's receptionist, I backed up and dialed.

She answered on the first ring. "Tabby, hi!" Her sixteen-year-old enthusiasm always came through in her greetings.

"Listen, I know Olivia isn't too happy with you right now, but any chance you could take my shift at The Heirloom this afternoon?" I asked. "I know I'm putting you in an awkward position, but I'd owe you big time."

Katie didn't even hesitate with her answer. "Of course I will, Tabby. If this has to do with an investigation, and especially if it has to do with that Reg guy, which I know you can't tell me, but if it does? I'm all over it!"

I thanked her, and reminded her to try to keep her pressured questions to herself for today, as I didn't want to see her get herself into trouble, especially if Reg was dangerous. I reminded her to call me if she needed me and hung up.

When I looked back up at Jay, he was scribbling a mess of notes. I looked to Pepper, playing with her sea glass, and she said, "I think I have an idea."

Chapter Twenty-nine

AT FIRST I FELT frustrated when Pepper's idea had nothing to do with Reg Carlson. But the more I thought about it, the plan might help us get to the bottom of some big secrets in this town.

As she explained more of what she had in mind, Jay and I listened closely.

"I want to know what your local mayor has against the witches. How long has he been in office?" she asked Jay.

"Just over a month." Jay looked like his mind was turning over this. "But he ran last election, too. At that point he lost, but I always figured it was because the town is quite divided over the witches. Mayor Herschel just kind of let them do their thing, but Matthew Kelsey was really cozying up to them for support on his first run at mayor."

This seemed contrary to everything we'd been learning about him lately. Then again, he had been letting the witches use his mansion for years for their haunted house. "But he didn't win," I said, stating the obvious. "And so he figured he should distance himself during this latest campaign?" I looked at Pepper as I said the words, wondering if her sea glass was warming as much as mine was. As daughters of a senator, we knew all about how underhanded motives could surface during a campaign run.

"I was thinking we should set Marigold up to try and trap the mayor and make him show his true colors regarding the local witches, but I don't know. Marigold comes across as a loose cannon to me and I don't know if we could count on her to keep her cool."

She was right about that.

"Mayor Kelsey doesn't know me, though. I'll go in as a witch considering moving to town and bringing my witch friends. I'll pry about what happened to Donna on Saturday night and see how he reacts. I'll say I've been talking to Reg Carlson, and see where that leads."

I shook my head. I didn't want to put my sister in danger, especially if Mayor Kelsey really could be behind Aunt Lizzie's and Donna Davine's murders, but when Jay said, "It's a good idea," I couldn't disagree. "I'll hook her up with a wire and we'll stay close. He's not going to hurt her right here in the Town Hall and I'll listen in on everything that happens." He looked at me. "Plus, you and I can stay close."

My mind reeled over possibilities of what we were still missing. Had Mayor Kelsey blamed Aunt Lizzie for his loss in the previous election? Had Aunt Lizzie trusted him, or had the power struggle among the witches flared up because of their concern over governmental powers? Maybe the witches had all been trying to protect the town in their own way. Or maybe I was simply reaching again, in order to think the best of the people I knew and cared about.

I was desperate for some answers, so desperate, apparently, that I was willing to let my sister walk into the front lines.

Jay dropped us off at the marina, while he went to the station to pick up some eavesdropping equipment.

"The thing is," Pepper said, following me to the *Lady of Fortune* with Sherlock in her arms, "I have to go in there *looking* like a witch. It has to be obvious."

"Right." I nodded. "So you'll wear some of Aunt Lizzie's clothes."

When I'd packed up Aunt Lizzie's long flowing dresses and gaudy jewelry almost eight months ago, it had been sad to look at every single piece. Now, with Pepper here, it was bittersweet.

Master would have wanted her things used to catch a killer in Crystal Cove. One last grand gesture for town.

I couldn't argue one bit with Sherlock's sentiments.

We made an appointment for two p.m. at the Mayor's Office, and Pepper gave the name Esmerelda Pepper on the phone. I had to bite back a laugh, because she was really good at this. Not only that, but she truly looked the part in my aunt's long sea foam green muumuu with a dozen sparkly necklaces. I helped her tease out her brown hair and soon this didn't look one bit like the academic and straight-laced sister I'd grown up with.

Jay knocked and walked aboard the houseboat and immediately grinned with delight. "This is going to work. This is definitely going to work."

Pepper nodded. "Good. Because we have a killer to catch."

Chapter Thirty

Jay and I sat in his car around the corner from the Town Hall, huddled over the laptop that was hooked up to the microphone Pepper had attached under her dress, while she went inside.

"I'm scared," I told him honestly. "Pepper's never done anything like this before."

Jay put a hand on mine on the console. "We're right here listening, Tabby. If anything even sounds remotely like it's about to go sideways, I'll get in there right away. Thom is also on his way over.

He's going to go into the Town Hall café, just to be a little closer."

That made me feel better, and so did hearing Pepper's voice a minute later through the laptop.

"Hellooo there. Esmerelda Pepper to see the Mayor, please." Her voice sounded nothing like the unassuming girl she was. In fact, she sounded a lot like Marigold.

As if Jay could read my mind, he turned to me and whispered, "See? She sounds just like Marigold."

Seconds later, Pepper introduced herself to Mayor Kelsey. I didn't know the Mayor well. I'd been to his acceptance speech in November, and he'd been in the café once while he was campaigning, but I'd never heard his voice as clipped as it sounded right now.

"Yes? What can I do for you, Miss Pepper?"

"I'm visiting from Portland," she said. "And I've been hearing conflicting stories about Crystal Cove. I was considering relocating here, but before I put a down payment down on a house, I wanted to make sure this was a good place for a young witch to settle." As she went on, her voice wavered in and out of its Marigold-esque accent, but I hoped I was the only one who knew Pepper well enough to recognize that.

"So you have not put down a deposit anywhere yet?" he confirmed.

"No, but I've been talking to Reg Carlson about a place just outside of town near the water. Do you know Mr. Carlson? Is he a reliable source?"

I was impressed with how quickly Pepper was getting all the pertinent questions into the conversation, but I could tell it was only her nerves wanting to get herself out of there. Sensing her nerves made me twice as anxious.

"Let's just back up the cart there, Miss Pepper. Before you go looking for a good realtor, there are some things you should probably know about the witch coven of Crystal Cove."

Realtor? Maybe I'd been right, and he did work, at least part time, in real estate. "I thought you said he worked in transport?" I whispered to Jay.

He nodded, but kept his mouth shut as Pepper spoke again.

"Oh no! That sounds serious. Please, tell me everything, Mayor."

Mayor Kelsey cleared his throat. "I don't know if you've heard, but we had a death of one of our local witches, just this past weekend. Plus, two of them died in the spring."

He was talking about Aunt Lizzie and Maple May, who I'd almost run over on my way into Crystal Cove so many months ago. And when he put it like that, it *did* sound like an ominous place for a young witch to move to.

Mayor Kelsey went on. "They don't get along within the community or even within their own coven. They say they care about Crystal Cove, but when push comes to shove, all they care about is using the town to make themselves more powerful. Always asking for special concessions, always assuming their agenda matters more than anyone else's. They claim they are here to help, but they don't even like to help each other. I've heard recent stories about some of them even sending each other death threats."

"Oh my!" Pepper said, truly sounding shocked.

"No, Miss Pepper. If I were you, I'd look farther south for somewhere to settle. Perhaps in California."

"Oh dear. Well, I really had my heart set on Crystal Cove, and you see, it's not only for me. I have a dozen witch friends in Portland who are looking for a small town to take over, er, I mean, settle into. Perhaps with all of us here we could change the witch vibe in town here."

"What? No—" he started to say, and his tone had grown angry, but Pepper spoke over him.

"You've been very helpful, Mayor, but I think I should speak with Mr. Carlson a little more before making my final decision."

"Who is this Mr. Carlson you keep talking about?" The mayor sounded farther away, like Pepper had made her way to the door of his office. I sucked in a breath, so ready for this conversation to be over.

"You don't know him?" Pepper asked, and I had to admit, it truly sounded like he didn't.

"I have no idea who he is, but I'll tell you this much. He's no friend of Crystal

Cove if he's trying to increase the witch population of our quiet little town."

"Oh. Okay…" Pepper sounded more unsure than she had during the entire conversation. I wanted to get her out of there, as Mayor Kelsey sounded like he was getting angrier and angrier. "But Mr. Carlson says he knows you. Mr. Reg Carlson?"

"I have no idea who that is." Again, the Mayor's words sounded true. "But I'll tell you what I'm going to do, Miss Pepper. Before you make a final decision about moving here and inviting all of your witch friends, I'm going to call my head engineer, Mr. Henry McGill, and have him take you across to where the witch died this past Saturday night. He can explain to you what happened. Maybe when you see it for yourself, you'll realize this town isn't safe for you and your friends."

The last part of his sentence repeated over and over again in my head, sounding more like a threat every time I heard it.

"Now, if you'll wait in my reception area for just a few minutes, I'll have Henry meet you there."

The second I heard Pepper's agreement, I was chattering nonstop to Jay. "We can't let her do it! Henry McGill is the engineer who rigged the flying stunt in the first place. And now he has access to a boat? What if he's been Matthew Kelsey's accomplice this whole time?"

Again, Jay placed a hand over mine. But then a second later, he was starting his car.

"What! No, we can't leave her here!" I said.

"We're not," Jay told me, his voice calm and filled with authority. "We're going with her."

Chapter Thirty-one

BEFORE JAY TOLD ME what he was thinking, he was on his radio with Aaron. "Pepper will be on the move soon with a man named Henry McGill. Keep a close tail on them. I'm expecting them to head to either the marina or the boat launch at Locality Brewery. I need to know which, and I need you to keep your eyes on them."

Aaron wasn't great at taking direction, but thankfully he agreed, and as soon as Jay clicked off, he looked at me. "Is Frank at the marina today?"

I nodded. "I think so." I'd seen his feet sticking out from working on the engine of a boat when Pepper and I had gone back to get her changed.

"Good. We're going to need his help."

We were too far away from the Town Hall by this time to hear Pepper. Only static came through the laptop. "I wish there was some way to get word to Pepper, to let her know we're watching her and won't leave her alone."

"She'll know, Tabby. Trust me, your sister knows how much you love her and how protective you are."

I took a deep breath and tried to believe him as we parked in the marina lot and rushed down the wooden steps to the wharf.

"Frank!" I called.

"We need to get a boat and get out of here quickly, in case Henry also heads over here to board one," Jay told me, just as Frank appeared, standing up in the small motorboat he was working on. "We have a situation. I need a boat that Tabby and I can take out immediately."

Frank looked between me and Jay. I didn't know who he trusted more, but his trust in one of us was enough to make him nod, and rush to his office for a set of keys. As we followed him, another worry ate at me. "What if he sees our boat on the reef? Or what if he's taking her out to the barge?"

Jay nodded. "Those are good questions. Frank, we might need your assistance out there."

Frank sorted through about a hundred sets of keys on a rack above his desk. "The *Molly Maiden* is pretty quiet. It's not mine, but I'll top her up with gas later, and I'm sure the owner won't mind." He led the way out onto the docks and to a small new looking motorboat with *Molly Maiden* emblazoned on the side. "Just let me know what to do."

Jay quickly rattled off the highlights of the entire investigation.

Frank interrupted. "Wait, Henry McGill? He has a boat here at the docks. Right over there." He pointed to an older boat, docked near the outer edge of the marina, then he turned to me. "You met him. Saturday afternoon when your sister had first arrived."

My eyes widened as I recalled the man arguing with Frank over money he owed. I hadn't exactly met him, but hadn't Frank suggested he had gambling debt?

"Does he take his boat out often?" Jay asked.

Before Frank could answer, I added, "Did he take it out Saturday?" He'd been on his way out of the marina when I'd seen him.

Frank nodded slowly. "He came by to get his keys Saturday afternoon. I'd been tempted to hold them for ransom until he paid his docking fees, but finally when he argued that he'd pay me within the week, I figured I might as well let him have one last joy ride, whether or not he stiffed me in the end." Frank started up the engine on the Molly Maiden, and it truly was quiet. "He said he'd be bringing it back late Saturday night, but he'd be sure to shut the motor off well away from the marina, so not to disturb anyone in the houseboats."

Jay explained everything we had learned, and Frank shook his head in disbelief the entire time.

On the boat ride over to the reef, Jay looked worried. So worried that it was making my stomach ache. "You think he's going to hurt Pepper, don't you?" I had to ask.

"What? No," he said quickly. "I just don't like involving so many civilians. If time wasn't of the essence, and if I thought there was any other way to find out the truth behind our murderous government officials, I wouldn't want

Pepper or Frank, or especially you anywhere near this investigation."

When we got out to the barge, Frank navigated to the left of it, so we'd be hidden from anyone on shore. It was stacked with several large containers, likely filled with recycled goods and had lots of places to hide. "I can drop you two at the reef and then tuck the *Molly Maiden* back over here," Frank suggested.

"But then how are you going to see if Henry all of a sudden comes this way and takes her to the barge, or worse, takes her out to sea?" My panic seeped out through my words.

"If I tie up the boat and board the barge, I'll be able to move around and have a great view in all directions."

When it was agreed, Jay and Frank made sure to connect by cell phone, so we could keep in touch about what was going on.

Minutes later, Frank dropped us off on the rear side of the reef, behind the lighthouse, just as Jay's phone pinged with a new text from Aaron.

"McGill's at the marina with Pepper. They're boarding his boat," Jay told me, reading from his phone. "Now let's find a good place to hide."

"I still don't like this," I said as I followed Jay along the rocky reef toward the lighthouse. "What if he just steers his boat out to sea to dump Pepper over the side?" My voice took on a manic tone as I could picture exactly this.

"If we see any sign of that, I'll radio Frank and he'll go after them." Jay's voice was calm, soothing, as if he knew I needed comforting.

"Frank's not a cop." Even though I made this argument, it was half-hearted, because I knew as well as anyone that if Frank took time to pick up Jay first, they might lose sight of Henry McGill's boat, or be too late before something happened to Pepper.

"Thom's connecting with Frank right now to get access to another boat. He'll also be on the water within minutes of McGill pulling away." He felt guilty about possibly putting yet another civilian in harm's way, I could hear it in his voice. "McGill is most likely to pull up exactly where Frank dropped us off. It's out of view of the mainland and there's an easy tie-up spot. I say we stay out of sight on the opposite side of the lighthouse."

"But that's too far from the door," I argued. "If he takes her inside the lighthouse, tries to make it look like she came over to investigate Donna's death and then jumped, what if we don't make it up to her in time?" I thought again of the narrow, winding staircase, only big enough for one person. I couldn't imagine Jay and I trying to rush up there at once, and quietly enough that we wouldn't be heard. What I could imagine was Henry McGill hearing us and pushing Pepper out of one of the windows on the way up. "I think one of us should go up now. To the top."

I had to admit, I was hoping Jay would offer to do this, but he said. "It's a good idea. I should stay on the ground, so I can stay mobile in case McGill has a different plan."

I nodded, chewing at my lower lip.

Jay pulled an earpiece from his pocket. "It's going to be okay, Tabby. We're going to stop this guy and keep your sister safe." He slipped the earpiece into his ear, then stepped closer and attached a small black microphone to my collar, inside my jacket. Then he pulled me into a hug.

I took three deep breaths, but then was startled away from him when I heard the whirring sound of a motorboat.

It was time. Jay had to get out of sight, and I had a whole lot of stairs to climb.

Chapter Thirty-two

OUR FIRST GUESS WAS right. Henry pulled up to the reef right as I passed the first open-air window in the lighthouse. I made sure to stay out of sight, but could still make out his small old powerboat, as he hooked it to the tie-up, and then saw him help "Esmerelda" out of the boat without her getting her dress wet.

I shook my head at him, acting so careful. Could we be on the wrong track? But with that one inner question, my sea glass went ice cold against my collarbone, and I felt a palpable sense of danger. This was the only thing that made sense from all the disparate threads of this case.

What surprised me most was the sight of Sherlock, sitting on his haunches on the front seat of the boat. Pepper must have found him outside the Town Hall and claimed he had to come along with her.

It probably made her feel safer to have a companion along—even a cat. In truth, it made *me* feel safer, too. I headed for the second long, circular set of stairs.

I didn't want to take time to catch my breath, and I couldn't see them out the second window. I wondered if Jay knew where they were, and I whispered, "I'm at the second level and don't see them outside anywhere," in case that would help. I wished I had an earpiece, so he respond to me.

By the third level, I heard voices. My sister's was loud, still taking on the Marigold-type tone, but her fast words told me how nervous she was. "What a beautiful lighthouse! You know, I've always wanted to live by the sea, and I just know my witch friends would love it here just as much."

I cringed. If Henry McGill had similar grievances as the Mayor to the local witch population, I hoped Pepper wasn't making him angrier with her words—so angry that he might try to hurt her sooner rather than later.

His voice was quieter, and because of the echo within the lighthouse, I couldn't make out his words.

A minute later, I had tiptoed to the top level of the lighthouse, where Jay had pointed out the battery from the cable cutting tool. It was gone now, and only a tent card with the number 17 remained in its place.

"Oh, this is quite the hike," Pepper said, sounding farther away. "Please, let's stop a minute so I can catch my breath." She was stalling. She had no idea we were here to help, which hopefully meant Henry McGill also had no idea.

"There's a concrete bench right there, if you need to sit." Henry's voice was quieter, but I was glad to hear he thought there was no rush.

Unfortunately, Pepper decided this was a good time to pry further into Crystal Cove's outlook on the local witches. "It's a lovely town, absolutely lovely, and yet, I have this feeling that your Mayor Kelsey doesn't want me here."

I was too far away from Pepper to help if she got him riled up and he decided to hurt her. I looked at the downward spiral of stairs, and considered quietly descending them a flight to be closer in case she needed me.

"Mayor Kelsey's just doing what he has to do to take care of our town. There's been nothing but unrest from the local witch coven lately and he's finding a way to put an end to that."

"And you're helping him do that?" my sister asked.

It was all too vague. We needed him to admit to murder, not only for himself, but conspiring to commit murder with our town mayor.

As if my sister knew this, she said, "You know, I have a sense about things, and I also have a magical cat." Her words were getting closer, like she was ascending the next set of stairs. I thought about Sherlock and wondered if he'd made it off the boat. He didn't love the water and definitely would have had to have gotten his feet wet to get to shore. "I have a sense that something's not right about these three witches who have died. The whole way over here, my cat's been warning me that something's not right."

"But you came anyway?" They were now close enough that I could hear all of Henry's words as well as my sister's.

"Sometimes, it's worth putting yourself in danger to know the truth," my sister said, and I didn't know if she was getting less afraid as she climbed the lighthouse, or if she really believed this.

But I didn't want my sister in danger. That wasn't worth it for me.

Their voices were so close, though. I had to get out of sight. The top level had an outer platform, an easy place to hide, but the second I moved out there with the wind hitting me and the view of our entire town, a queasiness moved into my stomach. It was so far down. I swallowed hard and crouched in place.

"Well, good. As long as it's worth it for you," Henry told her. His voice sounded strained, like he didn't want to be doing this any more than the rest of us.

"Then tell me the truth about your town. We're all alone up here. No one else needs to know what kind of secrets you're keeping about the local witch coven."

"And what would you plan to do with that information?" Henry asked. His voice sounded right next to me now. They were on the upper level. "…If I tell you."

Pepper forced casualness into her tone. I could feel it, even if I couldn't see her. "I'll go back and convince my witches to find somewhere else to live, of course. If things in Crystal Cove are really as bad as you say they are."

I wondered if Pepper still thought she was on her own out here. It sounded as though she really was trying to talk her way out of this. And maybe it would even work.

"Our mayor has been working hard to get into power, no thanks to the local witch community. Everything is for the good of the town, even if you, as an outsider, can't see it that way. It's taken him five years of campaigning, and he's not about to let them interfere with his authority now. He knows that the witches need to be deconstructed from the top down. That's why you need a strong man like Mayor Kelsey in office. He tried causing division between them, to keep them from getting too strong, but that didn't work."

"How did he try to cause division?" Before Pepper's question was out of her mouth, the answer came to me.

"He sent death threats, trying to bring to light the unrest between the witches. Unfortunately, they didn't take them seriously. Those head witches have too much power. He's afraid of their magic, and I've seen firsthand that he's not wrong. Last year, I helped one of the local witches perform a similar stunt to the one that killed the witch last Saturday. I'd convinced her to go up into the mountains and try it where no one else could see. I didn't know if Mayor Kelsey's concerns were valid, as the local witches had always seemed harmless to me. But then this witch, she levitated right off the wire. She flew in the air, and I couldn't believe my eyes. I clipped the wire when she was airborne because I truly believed she would fly right over to me and thank me for my faith in her magical abilities. When she fell to the ground, I couldn't believe my eyes, but this time because of her frail humanity."

"You killed her?" Pepper's voice sounded small. I was fighting the urge to sob at the revelation of how Lizzie had died.

"I never meant to do it." Henry McGill's words were tense, but also possibly remorseful. I couldn't be sure. "Kelsey had asked me to keep tabs on the two main witches in town. Told me if one of them got hurt, he'd pay me well for it. When I called and told him what had happened, he helped clean up the situation."

Clean up my aunt's death. Make it look like a suicide.

"I can tell you this: You should never have come to Crystal Cove. Now you know the truth. I hope it was worth it for you."

"The truth? What about Saturday? What about the other witch?" Pepper's voice came out in a squeak.

"Saturday? You mean the witch Kelsey blackmailed me into killing?" A long silence followed. Pepper had talked all the information we needed out of Henry McGill, but now what? How did we safely get ourselves off of the top of this lighthouse?

"I mean, you don't have to tell me anymore about it," she sputtered. "I'm sure I could find somewhere else to live if you just take me back to shore." Her voice was getting shakier and shakier, as if only now she was realizing what she was getting into.

"The thing is..." Henry said, and his voice was more assured than I'd heard it. "I don't believe you. And Mayor Kelsey is definitely not going to believe you, and so it's time to make sure you never step foot back in our town again."

Chapter Thirty-three

"No!" At Pepper's sudden shriek, I could no longer think about what I was doing or how to keep us both safe. I stood from my crouched position and raced to the inside lighthouse platform.

Or, I tried to. But Henry McGill was already forcing my sister through to the outside platform. The second he set eyes on me, his gaze darted in a hundred directions, looking for others, but my gaze was focused on only one place: the knife he held at my sister's throat.

"You don't have to do this!" I put my flat palms out toward both of them, to try to keep them as far from the chest-high ledge around the top of the lighthouse platform as possible.

But it wasn't working. A second later, I felt the ledge against my back, as he forced my sister toward me. Toward the ledge. "Why? Why do you think you have to help Mayor Kelsey kill people?" My words sounded frantic and shaky, and I doubted Jay could make them out from below, but hopefully, he at least knew we were in trouble.

Then again, by the time he ascended the hundreds of circular stairs, Pepper and I would both be dead.

"Why?" McGill's question came out in a tight squeak. "I'm sure you heard everything while you were up here hiding." His voice started out angry, but was quickly taken over by a heavy remorse that brought all the sadness I'd been keeping at bay to the surface. "Kelsey knows what I did to Lizzie. I owe him. I have to do what he says."

"But if you let him keep blackmailing you, he'll never stop." My voice was shaky, as much from holding back tears as from my fear. My sea glass warmed with my words. "He'll hold more and more over you."

Henry let out a humorless laugh. "I know you think I'm evil, but I'm only trying to take care of my family. It started with a little debt repayment, but now Kelsey has so much dirt on me, I have no way to argue. And trust me, he'll do *anything* to make sure he comes out on top."

Our dad had been in politics as long as Pepper and I had been alive. We knew about underhanded dealings. We'd grown up knowing to walk away from whispered conversations, and to not ask questions. But our dad had not been a murderer.

"Blackmail will never end well," I said, pleading with Henry. "But tell the police everything you know about Kelsey, and they can go easier on you." I honestly didn't know if this was true, and did I even want an easier sentence for the man who had killed Aunt Lizzie? "Put Kelsey behind bars so he won't be able to hurt your family, because if you let him get away with this, I promise you, he eventually will." I didn't mention the fact the Henry McGill would still be in prison. Even if he'd felt forced into it, he'd committed murder—at least one count of murder and one count of manslaughter—that we knew of.

"No." He shook his head. "This is it. We killed the two head witches and as long as we stop you from bringing any others to town, this will be the last time, and then I never have to leave my family and go to prison."

Pepper finally found her voice again. "You really think that's going to happen? You think all of a sudden, Kelsey will be done with you and stop making you do his dirty little *favors*?" Pepper's voice became stronger as she spoke. "We're proof that that's not the way it's going to go."

Henry's knuckles whitened around the knife at her neck. As he pushed her even closer to me, I tried to imagine his plan. He couldn't strong arm both of us at once to get us over the ledge. We might be able to fight him off, or at least threaten his plan.

He had to slice my sister's throat if he wanted to kill us both. The only reason he hadn't done it already was because he was having trouble stomaching that part.

"You don't want to do this. I know you don't." I forced my softest, most coaxing voice. "Besides, you don't really owe the mayor anything. He didn't clean up after Lizzie's death. He just took the credit for someone else's work."

His gaze darted back and forth between me and the ledge. He was working up the courage, and one wrong move on my part might make him go ahead with it.

With every word I spoke, I was paying close attention to my warming sea glass.

Before I could think of any other words, though, a sound from inside the top platform of the lighthouse surprised us all. Had Jay already made it up to the top to save us?

Before I could figure it out, Pepper used the distraction while Henry was looking toward the door to push him backward, and shove the knife from her neck.

Without a second thought, I rushed forward and pushed him. My knee came up and made contact with his stomach, and a second later, he tumbled backward and fell onto the stone floor, the knife clattering from his hand.

Pepper held him by an arm as he tried to scramble toward the knife. I was faster, though, and in a second, I kicked it over the lighthouse ledge.

Pepper had Henry's arm pinned under her foot now, but seeing the knife launch out of view was the moment that seemed to knock the fight out of him. "Noooo!" He whimpered as if he saw the consequences of all of his actions, flashing before his closed eyes.

"Yes," I told him. "And Detective Jameson has heard your entire confession, so it's over, Mr. McGill."

I looked toward the doorway into the top platform of the lighthouse, but Jay didn't step through it. I looked down to see...Sherlock.

My cat, saving the day one more time.

Chapter Thirty-four

HENRY WASN'T FIGHTING US. The second his knife had gone over the ledge, he'd given up the fight. Given up the idea that he'd somehow get out of this unscathed.

"Will you tell me more about what happened to Lizzie?" I asked, sitting down beside him. "She was my aunt."

He met my eyes for the first time, and I saw the intense sadness in them. "She wasn't a charlatan; I can tell you that much." The word made me think of Marigold, and I wondered if it had been Marigold he'd talked into going up into the woods alone to fly on a high wire, if things would have gone differently. "She was trying to help me figure out a way to clear my debts safely. I was so grateful for her kindness, and that's why I persuaded her to try the stunt by herself. I only wanted everyone to know how amazing she really was, without her having to share credit with any of those other supposed witches. She had a gift. And I took that away from you, from our town, from everyone."

It was another minute before Jay made it to the top of the lighthouse, his handcuffs already in his hands and ready to attach to Henry McGill, but hearing the topic of conversation, he held back.

"I really think she wanted to unite the town. It's my fault that everything's gotten so bad. If Lizzie was still around, she would have found a way to unite everyone."

I didn't doubt this was true. My warm sea glass helped me listen as he spoke, without allowing myself to get angry.

Eventually, when Henry had talked himself out about the genuineness of my aunt and the magic he'd witnessed, Jay read the man his rights as he attached the handcuffs and helped him to his feet. "One thing you'll be glad to know," he told Henry McGill, "is that our Mayor is already in custody. With your help, he's not going to conspire to hurt anyone else in this town."

Henry bowed his head. "I'm ready to take responsibility for my part and make sure he takes responsibility for his."

By the time we had boarded the *Molly Maiden* and returned to the marina, the place was full of police officers. Jay had been right to stay on the reef, where he had been able to communicate with Frank and Aaron and the rest of the local police, and have everything in place for our arrival back on the mainland.

It wasn't until Aaron had taken Henry McGill away that Jay turned and set eyes on me for the first time. He leaned his forehead against mine and said, "I couldn't have forgiven myself if he had hurt you." While he was close, he reached up to my neck, and I didn't know what he was doing until he unclipped the microphone from my collar that I'd forgotten was there.

"He didn't hurt me. I'm okay," I told him, as much as myself. "And Pepper's okay, too."

We both turned and looked toward Pepper, who was bent down and cooing over my heroic cat.

"And so is Sherlock," Jay said. "Do you think that cat would be willing to join our local police force?"

I chuckled as Jay pulled away. The dock had emptied of police officers and onlookers, but Pepper and Frank looked in no hurry to go anywhere. I think we were all still trying to catch our breath.

"Good luck with that," I told him, jokingly. "That cat, as heroic as he is, has a mind of his own."

By later that day, while Pepper had fallen into a deep afternoon nap to get over the stress of the morning, I was the opposite, and couldn't sit still. I scrawled a note for her, and headed for the café, figuring I could take over for Katie, so she wasn't stuck dealing with Olivia's gruffness toward her.

Now that I knew Reg Carlson wasn't a murderer, I wasn't quite as concerned about looking out for Olivia's safety, although I did want to be around in case she decided she wanted to talk.

I walked through the café door to see Katie's wide smile behind the counter and a half a dozen customers waiting to order. Folks in Crystal Cove were fairly understanding if they had to wait in line due to a sudden influx of coffee lovers, and they must have found our coffee and food items worth the wait, because they kept coming back—lineup or not.

I slipped quickly behind the counter, asking, "What can I get started?"

Katie had tried to refuse my help the first week she began working at the café, but when I'd convinced her of how she'd feel watching me struggle through a rush, she got over it and hadn't argued since. "One large skim latte, a London Fog with the orange twist, and a small mint mocha."

I nodded and got to work. Twenty minutes later, the line had dwindled down to nothing and we finally got a chance to say hello to one another.

"I thought you couldn't make it in?" she asked.

As usual, I didn't want to blab police details before they'd been officially announced. But I couldn't help the glow of pride that came over me at her question. Even if I couldn't share about it, we had caught the people who had conspired to commit two murders, including my aunt's, this morning. Pepper and I had helped make Crystal Cove a safer town.

I grinned and told her, "I got done earlier than planned." *And somehow stayed alive,* I added in my head silently, now almost giddy with the realization that Pepper and I were both safe, as was Rachael, and all my witchy friends and acquaintances. "How was it when you came in? How was Olivia?"

"Strangely quiet and distracted," Katie told me as she wiped up the counter. "In fact, if I hadn't told her that I was replacing you, I'm not sure she would have noticed. She didn't even get upset about it."

"Really?" That surprised me. Olivia could dig her heels in. If she'd wanted to keep Katie away from Reg a few days ago,

I wondered if the fact that she was happy enough to have Katie working this morning meant that he'd left town. But before I could ask, Katie answered that for me.

"I'm glad you're here, though. Olivia said something about a lawyer appointment. Said Reg Carlson was going to be by at four-thirty, and if she wasn't back in time, to ask him to wait for her."

I checked the time on my phone and it was almost that time now. I was also glad I was here, although I didn't relish the idea of having to give the guy a message from Olivia. I'd sooner tell him to get lost and leave her alone.

I hadn't had a lot of time to consider what I'd overheard of his phone call outside, but he clearly was planning something sneaky. The problem was getting Olivia alone and making her listen to reason.

As I stared at Katie, wondering if the two of us together would be able to talk some sense into Olivia, the door chimed and I looked over to see the man himself.

Reg stalked through the door, paused a couple of feet into the café, and looked from one end to the other. In less than five seconds, he took in Olivia's absence and turned back toward the outside.

Everything in me wanted to let him go, but a sudden pulse of warmth from my sea glass made me blurt out, "Excuse me? Mr. Carlson?"

He turned slowly back toward me. His jaw tightened, but he didn't respond.

"Olivia's running late from an appointment, but she'll be right along. What can I get you to drink while you wait?"

He paused, twisting his lips to the side as he considered this. He glanced at Katie, but only for a second. Then he walked for the counter. "I'll just take a black coffee."

We didn't get many orders for black coffee in Crystal Cove, but I poured him a cup and passed it over. As usual, there were several witches taking up most of the rear of the café. When Reg saw this, he re-angled himself to an empty table for two that was as far as he could get from both the witches and our serving counter.

As soon as he sat and glanced back in our direction, Katie and I jolted and feigned busyness. The whole time I was cleaning the espresso maker, I was trying to come up with the words I could say to the man in order to get him to leave Olivia alone, once and for all.

But then I second guessed every word that came into my head, because I knew without much consideration that Olivia would not easily forgive me for interfering in her love life.

Before I could give this too much thought, Olivia strode through the café door, clearly rushed and frazzled, but on a mission. I could see it in her eyes. She held a manila envelope in her hands, but that wasn't what immediately grabbed my attention. It was the gleaming diamond that sparkled from the ring finger of her left hand.

Oh no. I was too late to talk her out of anything.

Olivia didn't stop to speak to me or Katie, but headed straight for her fiancé. I could barely even think the word, and I reached up to fiddle with my sea glass, searching frantically for anything I could say or do to stop this. But my sea glass now remained cool, as if telling me I didn't have any part in this.

Katie was more nonchalant than I, and continued wiping counters, while keeping an eye on Olivia and Reg. I, on the other hand, stood staring like a deer in the headlights.

But, strangely, neither of them noticed. Olivia passed the manila envelope to Reg, and that seemed to take all of his attention. His scowl deepened as he opened it and pulled out some papers. I couldn't hear any of their words from my place at the counter, but then again, they didn't seem to be talking.

Olivia sat back in her seat and crossed her arms, watching Reg as he read whatever was on the papers in front of him.

He looked up and shook his head at her. Then, suddenly, he seemed to have plenty to say.

He dropped the papers and held out his palms as he appeared to plead with her. Olivia didn't say a word in response. She only pulled a pen from her purse and laid it on top of the papers.

Then she sat back to wait.

Seconds passed, then minutes. Reg continued to talk, while Olivia didn't say a single word. When Reg's words eventually ran out, Olivia only had one single response for the man. She pulled the ring off of her finger and set it down on top of the papers.

Reg stared at her for a long beat. Then he helped himself to the ring, stood, and hurried for the café door.

Olivia didn't watch him go. She stared down at the papers in the middle of the table like she couldn't tear her eyes away. I scooped a mug full of pear cider from the slow cooker—her favorite drink—and she still hadn't moved by the time I brought it over to her.

I set the cider in front of her and took the seat that Reg had vacated. I set my hand on her arm and she finally looked away from the papers and up to me. Tears brimmed the bottoms of her eyes.

"I was hoping it wasn't true. But I had to honor Donna's memory and at least look into what she believed."

"What did she believe?" My words were gentle. I glanced down at the papers, which had the heading: PRENUPTIAL AGREEMENT.

"She thought he was only after my café, after the land because of an old folktale that says there's buried treasure underneath it." She chuckled wryly and shook her head. "I've been approached by a lot of wingnuts over the years, trying to buy my café and convinced it would make them rich, but I've never had someone willing to *marry* me to get it."

"Buried treasure? Really?" I had to admit, I wasn't as unbelieving as Olivia seemed to be. I'd seen enough of the unfathomable in Crystal Cove that it wouldn't have surprised me one bit if Olivia was sitting on some long lost treasure. But if she didn't care to dig up her business and look for it, who was I to challenge her on it?

She nodded. "There are lots of stories about this town. But this place, this café, it's what I've always wanted. It's the real treasure to me, and I'm not going to sell it. I'm also not going to give it away through marriage."

I felt a sense of solidarity with her. When I'd first arrived in Crystal Cove, I'd been in search of external validation. I'd wanted to prove myself to my boss, to my father, to the world. In the end, it was the town and the people here that meant the most to me, and even if I didn't have much that the world would recognize, I felt a sense of rightness in my life now. I felt as though I'd at least begun to uncover my own treasure.

"I'm glad to know you could see through him," I told her honestly, as Katie came by to drop off a slice of blueberry coffee cake for Olivia, along with a napkin which Olivia immediately used to wipe her eyes.

She nodded. "You two definitely helped. I'm sorry I pushed away your well-meaning advice. I just... I didn't want to believe it."

"We're glad to know you're okay," Katie said, and moved back to the counter quickly. She probably still felt as though she'd overstepped with her boss. But I knew Olivia. She'd need a little time to get over what had happened, but then she'd be sure to show her appreciation to both of us.

"Is he out of your life for good?" I asked.

She nodded, slowly. "I've never seen somebody so scared of a piece of paper and a pen."

This made us both laugh.

"Where did you get off to this morning? Katie said you needed her to take over your shift."

"I thought I did," I told her, honestly. "I was busy trying to keep someone else in town safe." It was the most I could allude to without getting into the whole truth.

"You're pretty good at that, huh?" Olivia said, taking a bite of her coffee cake and looking like she was already getting over the heartache of her lost fiancé.

This was a question I no longer had any trouble answering. "Yeah, I think I am," I told her, and as my sea glass warmed around my neck, I knew it was more than simply something I was good at. It was our family legacy. And now my sister was here to make sure I wasn't alone in figuring it out.

The End.

Epilogue

Pepper and I barely saw Jay for the next twenty-four hours, as the entire police force dealt with not only the paperwork involved in arresting such a public figure and his accomplice, but the social fallout of the deception. People in Crystal Cove weren't the same. Every person who had come through the café doors had seemed jumpy, on edge, and had given their neighbor a side-eye untrusting glance.

It felt as though it was going to take a long time to come back from this.

And yet, both Pepper and I felt sure that Crystal Cove would eventually become better for it. Safer. A stronger community.

We Facetimed with our parents from the boat at dinner time on Christmas. They were unhappy that we weren't willing to make the drive to Portland to be with them in person, but together we put up a united front and told them we'd plan to be back soon for a visit.

I wasn't sure I meant that promise, but I only knew that now wasn't the time to run away from Crystal Cove. It needed me. It needed us.

"I'm just glad the two of you are together," Mom said, and I felt like she meant it.

"Where's Zach?" I scrutinized my laptop screen to try and see around the elaborate feast on our parents' dining room table. Zach, our older brother, was a lawyer whose number one client was our dad and his political office.

"Still working," Dad said, and even though he was at the far end of the table, and I couldn't see him well, I detected a note of pride in his voice. "We'll save him a plate."

I pulled back out of view of my webcam and rolled my eyes at my sister. We were both being given a guilt trip for not coming home, while Zach was given all the praise for working straight through Christmas. Still, he was under our father's thumb, and I would not have traded places with my brother for all the money and praise in the world.

Pepper and I had been too tired to cook a turkey dinner, but Olivia had made some savory puff pastry treats filled with turkey, stuffing, and cranberry. She'd insisted we help ourselves to the leftovers before closing up the café tonight, and they were currently giving off a wonderful aroma from my small oven.

"Your table looks empty," our mom observed, a note of sadness in her voice.

"There aren't many places to set the laptop up," I told her, and Pepper added, "Don't worry, food's in the oven."

Again, I had to pull back from the webcam to hide my grin.

Soon enough, our parents wished us a Merry Christmas and let us sign off. We both slumped back in our chairs as soon as I closed the laptop lid.

"Phew! Glad that's over," Pepper said.

I had never realized how much camaraderie I had with my sister. I knew I should encourage her to go back to school and finish her degree, but I also wanted to keep her in Crystal Cove for as long as she was willing to stay.

Besides, I sensed she needed the break from her studies. Maybe after a semester off, we'd talk about whether or not she planned to go back.

The timer dinged on the oven and Pepper went to go retrieve our puff pastry pockets. Once she had them on a plate, she looked back between me and our sad little empty table.

"You want to go for a walk with these?" she suggested.

I did. "That sounds perfect." It was cold out, but the snow that the weather report had been suggesting hadn't started up yet, and I felt like a walk in the crisp air would help lift the melancholy that was settling on me.

I'd worked hard at pasting a bright smile on my face at the café the last couple of days, but it had taken everything out of me. I was glad I didn't have to put up a front for my sister.

As soon as we were off of the *Lady of Fortune* and walking toward the mainland, a hot pocket in each of our gloved hands, Pepper told me, "I brought the blue crystal back from the café storage room yesterday."

She had been helping me at the café and had claimed tiredness, leaving early. I had thought I'd seen something sneaky in her eyes, but at the time I was too busy helping customers to dwell on it.

"And where is it now?" I asked.

"Back in the boat. In the glovebox, where you told me you used to store it."

It wasn't lost on me that she hadn't even brought this up until we were well off the boat. She must have understood, at least to some degree, how much the jewel affected me. I glanced down at Sherlock's blue jewel as he scampered along behind us, wondering if I'd ever get as comfortable with a crystal that wasn't attached to my cat.

"And did it affect you? Did you feel anything from it?" I asked.

She shook her head, but this time didn't look bothered, so much as thoughtful. "I had an idea, though." I waited for her to go on. "You feel too much from it, and I feel too little. What if we tried working with it together? Maybe not for a murder investigation, you know, where our emotions are supercharged, but for something smaller, less heightened."

A warmth came over my sea glass as an idea came to me. "Aunt Lizzie was said to have owned more blue crystals. Maybe...if we learned to harness the power..."

"We could find them," we both said at once.

We'd been walking aimlessly, first along the rocky beach, and then up to Shoreline Drive. In an instant, our excited mood dampened when the Town Hall came into view. Not only did the memory of the mayor's actions dishearten us, but because of the town's tragedies, whoever was in charge now had made the decision to keep the Christmas décor unlit.

"It's so dark." Pepper said exactly what I was thinking, and hearing her words out loud made another strong melancholy wash over me.

My phone buzzed in my pocket, and I pulled it out to see an incoming call from Jay.

"Merry Christmas," he said when I answered. It was nice to hear his voice.

"You still at work?" I asked.

"Just finished up." He sounded happy, but he must have detected something in my tone, because he asked, "You okay, Tabby?"

I sighed. "Yeah, I'm fine. Pepper and I are out for a walk and the Town Hall is so dark. It just makes me feel so sad for our town, you know?"

His voice softened. "I do." I believed he, more than anyone else, could understand. "Are you two up for some company?"

I was, but he had been working a lot of long hours the last few days. "Shouldn't you go home and get some rest?"

"The Captain gave me tomorrow off. I can sleep in." When I told him I'd love the company, before hanging up, he said, "And let me see what I can do about those lights."

Pepper and I said we'd wait for Jay in front of the Town Hall. There were lots of cement ledges on the ocean side, and people often lounged around the area in the summertime, as it was a picturesque spot.

There was no one else out here and it was quiet and damp from the salty sea air, but I felt a little lighter knowing Jay was on his way. Before he showed up, though, another lone car drove in our direction down Shoreline Drive.

My gaze stayed on the car as it pulled up in front of the Town Hall. The man inside turned off his car and got out. Next thing I knew, he unlocked the front doors to the Town Hall and thirty seconds later, the entirety of the building was bathed in multi-colored lights.

I felt a little badly that Jay had taken this man away from his home at eight o'clock at night on Christmas night to drive down here and turn the lights on. But at the same time, my insides lit up almost as much as the building in front of us.

"We needed this." Pepper wrapped an arm around my shoulder and squeezed, bringing a nostalgic comfort I had missed. "And the town needs us, you know."

It wasn't a question, but I nodded anyway. I did know.

A warmth came over me and my sea glass as the man emerged from the building and locked it up again. I had to thank him.

I walked toward him and waved before he could get back into his car.

He hesitated but then walked in my direction. I met him halfway, and Pepper followed. I recognized him, like he may have been into the café once or twice, but I didn't know his name. I was about to rectify that.

"I'm Tabby." I held out my gloved hand for a shake. "And this is my sister, Pepper."

As he shook my hand, he told me, "Jay said our town could use some extra light tonight."

"Yes. Thank you for coming down here to turn them on. This is so much better, isn't it?" I motioned to the building.

The man assessed the Town Hall and then nodded. He still hadn't told me his name.

Before I could ask, Jay's sedan pulled down the street and right behind this man's car. As he got out, the man turned back and said, "Nice to meet you," nodding to me and Pepper and then heading back toward his car.

Jay, by this time, had pulled a guitar from his backseat. He called out, "No, please, Gary. If you don't have to rush off, stick around."

Gary? In a second I locked that name to memory. I wouldn't forget it.

But more importantly... Jay played guitar? Not only that, but it looked like he was going to play it now.

He moved over to us, first to Pepper, and he leaned in to give her a hug. Then he moved to me, hugging me longer and kissing me on the forehead. It wasn't the kind of kiss with Jay I'd been imagining lately, but it brought tears to my eyes, knowing how much he cared about me.

"When you told me how dark it was, and right around our town center, I figured maybe we should do something to fix that." He bent to unbuckle his guitar. "I called a few people. I hope you don't mind."

The tears in my eyes were seriously threatening to fall.

"We don't mind at all." Pepper answered for both of us as she touched her sea glass. Mine was toasty warm against my collarbone. This was right. This was exactly right.

As Jay sat on the cement ledge and started to play and sing "It's Beginning to Look a Lot Like Christmas," two other cars pulled up to the Town Hall and people got out. They pointed to the Town Hall's lights and then ambled toward us, smiles emerging on their faces. People who lived close enough walked over on foot, some carrying lawn chairs like they were planning to stay, others carrying hot beverages.

Within minutes, a crowd formed, and they joined in to sing with Jay.

Smiles appeared on faces all around us. Pepper stood to pick up Sherlock, and then she and I looked at each other, both with a hand on our warm sea glass necklaces.

We started to sing along.

Maybe, between Jay, Pepper, and I... and Sherlock, of course... Maybe it wouldn't take so long for Crystal Cove to come back, after all.

The End.

For more bonus epilogues, only available to subscribers, sign up for my newsletter at

https://www.subscribepage.com/

mysteryreaders

Turn the page for a sneak peek at Denise Jaden's Mallory Beck Cozy Culinary Capers, and after that, a couple of Tabby's favorite recipes!

Introducing... Murder at Mile Marker 18

Book 1 in the Mallory Beck Cozy Culinary Capers

AN UNLUCKY AMATEUR SLEUTH, an adorable cop, and a cat with a hunch...

If anyone had told Mallory Beck she would become Honeysuckle Grove's next unschooled detective, she would have thought they were ten noodles short of a lasagna. Her late husband had been the mystery novelist with a penchant for the suspicious. She was born for the Crock-Pot, not the magnifying glass, and yet here she is elbow deep in fettuccine, cat treats, and teenagers with an attitude, the combination of which lands her smack-dab in the middle of a murder investigation.

Maybe she should have thought twice about delivering a casserole to a grieving family. Maybe she should have avoided the ever-changing green eyes of her seventh-grade crush—now the most heart-stopping cop in town. Maybe she should have stopped listening to the insightful mewls of her antagonistic cat, Hunch, who most likely wants her to be the town's next murder victim.

Whatever the case, Mallory Beck got herself into this investigation, and she has a distraught teenage girl counting on her to deliver the truth.

Turn the page to read the first two chapters...

Murder at Mile Marker 18

Chapter One

THE WIFE OF A war correspondent or a fighter pilot or even a venomous snake milker (yes, there is such a thing) might expect to be a widow at twenty-eight, but certainly not the wife of a novelist.

And yet here I was, learning how to live life in the oversized house, in a small West Virginia town we settled into only a year ago—alone. To be fair, I hadn't done much in the way of living in the last eight months since Cooper died, but after an offhand comment from my sister about me being under great threat of becoming a cat lady, I was determined to start today.

Being a cat lady wouldn't be so bad if the cat I'd inherited didn't loathe me.

I swung my legs out of Cooper's black Jeep and did a little hip shimmy to straighten my skirt as I stood. Picking out clothes this morning had been about as difficult as choosing between cake and pie (no one should ever have to make that choice). What does one wear that says, *I'm fine, just fine, and I haven't been moping around my dark house for the last eight months, nope, not me, but nonetheless, please, keep your distance?*

Even though it was the middle of August, I had settled on a black skirt with the tiniest of polka dots and a light cornflower blue blouse with matching pumps and a headband that pulled my in-need-of-a-trim bangs back. It didn't spell out the last eight months of my life, but it did the job in making me feel tidy and unapproachable. My coffee-brown hair fell halfway down my back now, full of split ends, but it actually didn't look half bad today for how many months it had been matted against my living room couch.

I strode for the church, the same one I hadn't stepped foot inside since Cooper's memorial service. Church had always been Cooper's thing. I'd gone along to play the part of the good wife but didn't spend too much time considering how I felt about God or how He felt about me. At least I hadn't before He decided to snatch my husband from me.

Two greeters in their mid-forties stood at the closest open glass doors—a man in a gray suit and a woman in an apricot summer dress. Thankfully, I didn't recognize either of them. I'd chosen this as my first big public outing because, at more than three hundred people, I figured our church was the one place I might get in and out of completely unnoticed. As I approached the greeters, though, the woman leaned into the man and whispered something.

I gulped. Apparently, this was how it would go: People would recognize me, remember Cooper, and not know what to say. Why, again, had I gotten out of bed this morning? There had to be at least one Netflix series I hadn't binged yet.

The woman at the door pasted on a bright smile as she turned back to me, just in time to say, "Good morning."

"Good morning," I murmured back, but my voice came out hard and crusty, like bread out of a too-hot oven, or like I hadn't used it in more than a week. Come to think of it, other than talking on the phone with my sister, I probably hadn't. My tone, at least, had the desired effect, and the greeters let me pass without another word.

My next goal was to make it through the lobby and into the sanctuary without garnering any other stares or attention. This part was not easy. All eyes followed me as I entered the church lobby, and I was pretty sure I wasn't just imagining it.

My late husband, Cooper Beck, had been a well-known mystery writer, so I was used to recognition. After only five years, I hadn't been married long enough to get used to this feeling of notoriety, and I guess I had assumed it would have died with Cooper.

Apparently not so. And not only that, but every single person nearby was scanning my body, probably taking in my too-bright cornflower blouse and thinking it inappropriate for someone in mourning, or noticing the tiny polka dots on my skirt, or wondering why I still wore black after so many months, or...something.

While I was lost in my warring thoughts, Donna Mayberry spotted me, at first only giving me a glance, and I thought I might make it into the sanctuary before actually having to speak to her. But then she did a double take, quickly followed by the head tilt of pity. By this point, I knew that look well. That look was why I had taken to grocery shopping and running errands at midnight instead of during the day like a normal person. At midnight, I could safely avoid the head tilt of pity.

"Mallory Beck?" Donna called with an arm straight up in the air, so any stray person in the vicinity who hadn't yet set eyes on me might do so now. "It's so nice to see you out!" she said loudly, calling public attention to my self-imposed isolation in only two seconds.

Donna had the kind of long legs that would be impossible to outrun. In fact, I blinked, and she was right there beside me. Donna was long everywhere—from her fingers to the dark, shiny hair that fell past her waist. She wore a summery yellow dress that touched the floor, and I had to wonder what kind of a store made clothes that would look long on someone like nearly six-foot Donna. Whether it was her hair or her stature or her clothes, though, Donna Mayberry always seemed to have a way of making me feel frumpy and underdressed.

Then again, maybe all these people would finally look at her instead of me.

Donna and Marv were one of the first couples Cooper and I had met when we'd settled into Honeysuckle Grove a year ago, and while Marv worked about sixteen hours a day, Donna naturally excelled at everything from shrub carving to Michelangelo-inspired nail design, and seemed to have a little too much time on her hands—time to know everything about everyone.

"How are you doing, honey? Is this your first time back at church?" Again with the head tilt of pity. Even though I doubted Donna could know I hadn't left my house in thirteen days, somehow her tone confirmed she absolutely did.

"First time, yes," I replied. No point in denying it.

She angled me away from the imposing stares and nudged me toward an alcove as though she could sense how much the staring bothered me. A second later, a tall, potted plant concealed us in the corner of the lobby, and I had just let out a breath of relief when Donna suddenly started pulling at my skirt.

I grabbed for my skirt and looked down in horror. Was Donna trying to undress me? Was this a bad dream? Maybe I was still sleeping soundly—or as soundly as one could beside a hostile cat while dreaming about being undressed in public.

But as I blinked and then blinked again, Donna held up a pair of beige control-top pantyhose she had peeled off the outside of my skirt to show me. A second later, she tucked them into the outside pouch of my gray leather purse.

"Oh!" I let out a loud noise, something between a yelp and a laugh. "Thank you!"

As I peeked around the plant, it seemed everyone had lost interest in us, thank goodness.

"Well, you'll have to sit with us." Donna straightened her own dress and looked down as though something equally embarrassing might have happened to her, but I was pretty sure we both knew that wasn't how the universe worked. I doubted Marv was here, so "us" likely meant Donna's gossip posse—that was what Cooper and I used to call them—but as Donna tugged my arm toward the far side of the lobby, a jolt of panic shot through me.

"Oh, I can't," I said, pulling away from her eight-tone sunset nails. "I'm, um, meeting someone, and I said I'd be sitting on this side." The first lie I could think of launched off my tongue. I just couldn't imagine sitting with Donna's posse and having them all whisper, "Yes, but how are you really doing?" fifty times throughout the service.

Donna looked to either side of me as though she might regard this mysterious person I could be waiting for. I could have continued with the lie. Said my sister was in town or conjured an imaginary friend or something to put her mind at rest. But I was suddenly just so tired from all of this interaction—the most I'd endured in eight months—and so I simply stood there staring at Donna like my brain had taken an extended vacation.

Eventually, she said, "Oh. Okay then. If you're sure?"

I nodded as she backed away, leaving me to my social anxiety.

A few more head tilts greeted me as I took my seat near the back of the sanctuary on the right, nice and close to the door. Thankfully, my chosen outfit—sans the sticky pantyhose—did its duty of keeping me mostly unapproachable. The church had rarely filled to capacity when Cooper and I had attended, so I had some confidence I'd have the back bench to myself. The only time I'd actually seen this place full was at Cooper's memorial service, but most of those were mystery fans and people fascinated with death, not people who had actually known him.

Soon, the service started with singing and then the pastor's invitation for people to donate and volunteer in any area they were able. Nothing had changed in eight months, apparently. Honeysuckle Grove Community Church still didn't have enough money in the building fund or enough people to host small group Bible studies in their homes. It seemed so very odd that while my life had been turned on its head, leaving me without a husband or a profession, every person around me seemed like a walking robot, pre-programmed for a life that would remain constant until their pre-determined time of death.

As though Pastor Jeff could read my mind, he started his sermon with, "We are not robots."

That was one thing I'd forgotten about church. Pastor Jeff had a great gift for storytelling. He usually started one of his stories with a bold and unusual statement, and then went on a long rabbit trail about his son's first crack at baseball or about that time he lost his luggage in a Taiwanese airport, but then brought it back around to that first bold statement in a way that made the entire congregation think, *Ah, I see what you did there!*

But today, I feared I didn't have the brain capacity to follow his breadcrumbs. He chattered on about what it meant to be part of a family and body parts working together and covering a multitude of sins. At least I had been correct about getting the back bench to myself.

I tuned out for a minute, or maybe it was more than a minute, because the next thing I knew, Pastor Jeff closed his Bible and bowed his head to pray.

I'd done it! I'd made it through the entire service. Okay, maybe I hadn't taken much of it in, but I'd spoken to an actual person, I'd sat here and proved I could act normal, and I hadn't drawn a single bit of attention to myself. Well, besides the part where I wore my pantyhose on the outside of my skirt.

"I'm sorry to have to tell you there's been a recent death in the congregation," Pastor Jeff said. At first, I expected all eyes to once again turn to me, but then quickly realized "recent" in Pastor Jeff's books meant something during the last two seasons. "This past Friday, August the thirteenth, Dan Montrose met his death in an unfortunate accident."

Pastor Jeff resumed bowing his head to pray for the family and their loss. His deep voice boomed with emotion and instantly made me feel like I'd gone back in time eight months. I could physically feel grief for this family I'd never even met, like a two-hundred-pound anchor in my stomach. Pastor Jeff went on to talk about the shock of the death and the wife and children this man had left behind, and because I couldn't bear the weight of the extra grief, I kept my eyes open and focused on our authoritative, if somewhat frazzled, pastor.

Pastor Jeff wore jeans and a beige button-down today. His hair was more in need of a trim than mine, which was saying something, but in every bit of his countenance, he oozed compassion. I wondered how overworked Pastor Jeff must be to take care of such a large congregation. It must involve a lot of stress for someone who cared so much. After Cooper died, Pastor Jeff visited me three times at the house, until I'd finally donned a face that convinced him I was doing fine, just fine, and didn't need a fourth visit. In truth, I probably *did* need that fourth visit, but even then, in the midst of my grief, I had somehow inherently known that I would be doing our overworked pastor a great favor by letting him move on to some other hurting soul within the church.

"Anyone?" Pastor Jeff said, and it took me a second to realize he had finished praying and now gazed over the congregation with his eyes pleading, as he often did at the beginning of the service when asking for volunteers. I had tuned out again. "Can anyone be the arms of this church body and deliver a casserole to these hurting folks, to help out this part of our church family?" He scanned the entire congregation a second time. "It doesn't have to be anything fancy."

He looked to the far side of the sanctuary where Donna and her gossip posse huddled whispering, and then in front of them to where the rest of the church staff sat. The church secretary, Penny Lissmore, let out such a large breath of disappointment, I could see her chest heave from across the large worship center. Pastor Jeff sighed as though admitting defeat to her and explaining telepathically that they'd have to add Casserole Delivery to the long list of things someone on the staff would eventually have to get to.

After Cooper died, I'd had at least a couple of casseroles delivered to me. That time was a bit of a haze, and I definitely didn't ponder at the time how much cajoling it might have taken to get someone to pick up a casserole at the store—they were the store-bought variety, I remembered that much—and bring it over to my house.

I got it. Approaching a grieving widow was probably near the bottom of most people's lists of favorite things to do, right below getting a root canal or having a wardrobe malfunction on your first day back at church. But for the first time, I understood how comforting those little acts of kindness could be.

While I was lost in my thoughts again, I didn't immediately notice the church secretary and an associate pastor look my way, followed by Pastor Jeff. His face broke into a smile that looked as though heaven had just opened and angels were descending right here on this side of the sanctuary.

"Mallory Beck!" he said, and I startled at my name. "I knew I could count on you. Thank you so much, Mallory. The Montrose family will really appreciate this."

I blinked as I clued in to what he was saying. And that's when I realized my hand was high in the air.

Murder at Mile Marker 18

Chapter Two

Two hours later, I stumbled through my front door, carrying more groceries than one person should be able to manage. As if to prove my point, as I kicked the door shut behind me, the bottom fell out of one of the brown paper bags in my right arm, and dried noodles scattered everywhere.

Hunch peeked around the corner to investigate. Cooper's cat generally snubbed his nose in my direction. Once in a while, he greeted me with a hiss—usually when I was already having a particularly bad day. My sister, Leslie, thought I should really take Hunch down to the SPCA if we didn't get along, but I couldn't get rid of Cooper's beloved cat. Of course I couldn't.

But we also couldn't stand each other.

Now he looked up at me as if saying, "This is new," about not only the noodles on the floor, but also about my overloaded arms. Generally, when I made a trip to the grocery store, I returned with one bag, maybe two. It didn't take a lot to feed a single person, especially one who rarely remembered to eat. Or a single person and a mourning cat.

Yes, mourning. I should take a step back and explain. You see, Hunch was not a normal cat. Hunch's personality was more dog-like than feline in many ways, and he had been every bit the ideal mystery writer's companion. The cat had only ever seemed to enjoy Cooper's company, and I hadn't taken it personally when Cooper was alive because they clearly fit together. When Cooper paced, Hunch paced right alongside him. When Cooper came up with a great plot idea and snapped his fingers, Hunch perched on his haunches right at Cooper's side to high five his owner. I kid you not. Or in this case, would you call it a low five?

I still didn't take Hunch's bristly nature to heart. It just disappointed me that we both missed Cooper terribly and yet we couldn't comfort each other through our grief.

But I could never fill the void Cooper had left in Hunch's life. I couldn't possibly stir up the kind of creative energy that new mysteries and their solutions brought with them. I'd been reading Cooper's novels nonstop for six months to keep what little he'd left behind close to me, and all it had taught me was that I'd lost someone brilliant. No wonder he'd had such a large fan base.

I dropped the intact grocery bags onto the kitchen counter and returned to clean up my mess. Hunch was still investigating, sniffing every inch of my torn grocery bag and its contents like a squatty feline bloodhound. He looked up at me and I swear he raised his eye whiskers on one side as if to ask, "What, exactly, are you up to?"

"I wish I was up to something more exciting," I told Hunch. Cooper had often talked to his cat, but for me, it had always felt strange, at least before today. "Just cooking up a casserole for some nice people who recently experienced a death in the family."

Hunch's fur pricked up on the word "death" and even though there was no story here, no mystery about what I planned to concoct in the kitchen, I figured it wouldn't hurt to let Hunch think differently.

"I'll have to figure out what to do now that I've wasted my noodles," I said, pacing a few times back and forth in our entryway and drumming my fingers on my chin. Hunch watched me for a few seconds. And then he joined me.

The truth was, I knew exactly what to do. And, in fact, purchasing the dried pasta noodles had been a cop-out on my part—barely a step above buying a frozen lasagna.

I didn't blame anyone else for opting for store-bought, of course. Other people had busy lives, while I had absolutely nothing on my agenda, besides getting out of bed and pouring a bowl of cat kibble. Also, most other people didn't have a culinary degree.

Half an hour later, my oven pinged to let me know it was preheated, but I still hadn't decided on a recipe. I had all the ingredients for a basic pasta recipe, but basic seemed much too boring when I hadn't had the opportunity to cook for anyone in eight months. I'd bought tomatoes, so I could flavor the pasta that way, but it still didn't seem good enough. Why hadn't I picked up some spinach? Maybe some saffron?

It ended up being three days and four trips to the grocery store later when I finally decided on a recipe I was happy with. I'd fried sauces and taste-tested a dozen different cheeses. I knew beyond any doubt that I was putting far too much thought into this, and yet I couldn't seem to stop myself.

Besides, once the casserole was cooked, that meant I had to actually deliver it.

But by Wednesday, I had finally worked up the courage and got out of bed by seven in the morning to get started—a time of the day I hadn't seen in many months.

Once again, I preheated the oven, mixed eggs, flour, and salt, and separated my dough into three balls. I blended my first ball with a dough hook and a cup of pureed spinach, the second with crushed tomato, and the third with some olive oil and a touch of saffron. By the time I rolled them all out onto my counter and sliced them into thin fettuccine noodles, I was perfectly pleased with the bouquet of edible colors.

Hunch had been lying on his chair at the kitchen table, chin on his paws, since I started. His eyes followed me throughout the kitchen as I asked myself questions aloud about my recipe and then answered them as if each one were a clue in a grand mystery.

For the first time in eight months, Hunch and I seemed to enjoy each other's company, and all at once, something felt very right about this decision to make a meal for this grieving family. The truth was, I never needed to work again if I didn't want to. Cooper had excellent life insurance, plus a steady stream of royalties from his books. But therein lay the problem—I didn't want to go back to working in a bustling kitchen, and yet I terribly missed cooking, as it never seemed worth putting much effort into the process for only one person. It would be so much easier to stop sitting around my big, lonely house, moping all day every day, if I had somewhere to be.

And now for at least one afternoon, I did.

I continued to ask questions aloud, like, "I wonder how the man died," and "I wonder how his wife is dealing with her grief," as I heated some oil in a saucepan over medium heat, to keep Hunch's attention. I warmed my crushed garlic in the oil until fragrant, added more freshly boiled and crushed tomatoes, and salt. By the time the sauce thickened, I had some chopped basil ready to add.

I grated some cheddar and tried it with the sauce, but quickly decided it lacked richness and added some gorgonzola. Then I layered the casserole into my best white casserole dish—pasta in three different-flavored mounds, then the sauce, a little extra sea salt, and finally the mixture of grated cheeses. I decorated the top with chopped green and yellow peppers for color.

I popped it into the oven and set it to bake twenty-five minutes. And then I raced upstairs to choose an outfit for today's special outing.

Buy Murder at Mile Marker 18 now to read on...

Recipe: Christmas Leftover Hot Pockets

IF YOU'RE LOOKING FOR something to make with your holiday leftovers other than turkey sandwiches and turkey soup, you'll love this yummy recipe! I make a double batch, and they all still disappear when I've barely taken them out of the oven. Feel free to switch up ingredients as you please—these can be a little different every time you make them.

Ingredients:

2 cups leftover turkey (shredded)

1 cup mixed vegetables

1 cup leftover mashed potatoes

1 cup leftover stuffing

½ cup leftover gravy

2 ready-rolled puff pastry

salt and pepper to taste

1 egg (to brush the pockets)

Instructions:

1. Preheat the oven to 180 degrees Celsius (350 Fahrenheit).

2. Mix the leftover ingredients with the vegetables in a bowl.

3. Roll the puff pastry, and cut it into 6 squares.

4. Add one tablespoon of the mixed turkey filling in the center of the pastry square, bring the corners of the pastry together to form a triangle, and press with a fork to

seal the edges. Repeat with all the pies.

5. Beat the egg, and brush each pie with it, then make 2 small cuts on top to allow the steam to be released while baking.

6. Line 2 or 3 baking trays with non-stick paper and bake for about 25 minutes until golden.

Notes:

Substitute whatever leftovers you have, and if you don't have turkey, try it without, or with chicken. Add cranberry for a bit of added sweetness. Enjoy!

Recipe: Slow-Cooker Pear Cider

INGREDIENTS:

8 medium pears, (choose your favorite or assorted types – Bosc, Red Anjou, Bartlett)

1 orange, peel with pith removed to avoid bitter flavor

3 cinnamon sticks

3 slices of fresh ginger

1 whole nutmeg

3 star anise

2 teaspoons whole cloves

6 cups water

⅓ cup maple syrup

Instructions:

1. Cut the pears and orange into quarters. Seeds, peels and stems are fine. Place the fruit in the bottom of your slow cooker

2. Add the cinnamon sticks, ginger slices, nutmeg, star anise, and cloves.

3. Fill to the top of the slow cooker with water, leaving 1/2-inch of space at the top. Cook on high heat for 3-4 hours or on low heat for 6-8 hours.

4. An hour before the cider is done cooking, use a potato masher to mash the fruit once it is softened.

5. Strain the pear cider through a fine-mesh strainer or cheese cloth into a clean pitcher or pot,

pressing on the solids to get all of the juice out of the fruit. Stir in the maple syrup until it is dissolved and serve hot.

6. Enjoy!

Reviews Matter...

Honest reviews help bring new books to the attention of other readers. If you enjoyed this book, I would be grateful if you would take five minutes to write a couple of sentences about it. You can find all the books in this series to leave reviews at the following link.

https://books2read.com/denisejaden

Thank you so much for your support. I couldn't do this without readers like you!

<u>**THE TABITHA CHASE DAYS of the Week Mysteries**</u>

Book 1 - Witchy Wednesday

Book 2 - Thrilling Thursday

Book 3 – Frightful Friday

Book 4 – Slippery Saturday

A Bookworm of a Suspect
Mystery Anthology (Including Book 5 – Dead-end Weekend)

<u>**The Mallory Beck Cozy Culinary Capers:**</u>

Book 1 – Murder at Mile Marker 18

Book 2 – Murder at the Church Picnic

Book 3 – Murder at the Town Hall

Christmas Novella – Mystery of the Holiday Hustle

Book 4 – Murder in the Vineyard

Book 5 – Murder at the Montrose Mansion

Book 6 – Murder during the Antique Auction

Book 7 – Murder in the Secret Cold Case

Book 8 – Murder in New Orleans

Find all the Mallory Beck novels at bit.ly/MalloryBeck!

Collaborative Works:

Murder on the Boardwalk

Murder on Location

Saving Heart & Home

Nonfiction for Writers:

Writing with a Heavy Heart

Story Sparks

Fast Fiction

Denise Jaden is the author of the Mallory Beck Cozy Culinary Capers and the Tabitha Chase Days of the Week Mysteries. She is also the author of several critically-acclaimed young adult novels, as well as the author of nonfiction books for writers, including the NaNoWriMo-popular guide Fast Fiction.

In her spare time, Denise acts in TV and movies and dances with a Polynesian dance troupe. She lives just outside Vancouver, British Columbia, with her husband, son, and one very spoiled cat.

Sign up on Denise's website to receive bonus content (you'll find clues in every bonus epilogue!) as well as updates on her new Cozy Mystery Series.

www.denisejaden.com

www.ingramcontent.com/pod-product-compliance
Lightning Source LLC
Chambersburg PA
CBHW050851210726
48290CB00004B/1183